"I'll take care of you, Catherine."

David's words seemed grim with determination.

Catherine laughed incredulously. "And it's all because you feel sorry for me, is that it?" she asked.

He shook his head, slowly turning his eyes to hers. "When you're ready, I'm going to marry you."

"You're *what*?" She shrank away from him—but not out of fear or lack of wanting to be near him. David Hungerford was a man one could lean on, but as for love....

"Don't you think I deserve someone who cares for me?" she cried.

"I can *take* care of you, Catherine," he said softly.

But it was not enough for Catherine. It could never be enough.

The Golden Puma

by

MARGARET WAY

Harlequin Books

TORONTO • LONDON • LOS ANGELES • AMSTERDAM
SYDNEY • HAMBURG • PARIS • STOCKHOLM • ATHENS • TOKYO

Original hardcover edition published in 1980
by Mills & Boon Limited

ISBN 0-373-02357-X

Harlequin edition published September 1980

CHAPTER ONE

Out in the canefields it was appallingly hot, yet Catherine continued to sit in the battered old utility watching the harvester cut a swathe through the tall, brilliantly green blades. Nowhere in the world did the cane grow taller or richer in sugar than the great canelands of North Queensland, and she responded to the sight and the incredible lushness with a sense of great oneness.

Beyond the endless sea of mauve-tipped waving plumes, away in the far distance, yet dominating the landscape, was an isolated cone-shaped mountain of solid tin that reared six thousand feet straight up out of the jungle plains. Today its summit was hidden by a billow of thick white cloud, the only cloud in the whole peacock sky.

It was breathtaking country and Catherine continued to sit with her tanned slender arms slumped over the wheel, contemplating the brilliant mosaic pattern of blue sky, green jungle and blood-red soil. In truth she was too exhausted to move, but the firing and then cutting of the cane held great drama for her. A ritual, centuries old, though the days were long gone when the kanakas, then the white men, hard-muscled and shining with sweat and blood, cut through cane twice their height with mighty strokes of the machete.

Now Australia led the world in the mechanical

cultivation and harvesting of the crop. The North *was* sugar, and above and beyond its importance as a major industry, it had been the means of developing and populating the far North of the giant State of Queensland. Directly or indirectly, hundreds of thousands of people depended on sugar for their livelihoods and many Queensland towns existed solely because of their association with the mills.

It was her world and she was happy in it. Had been happy. The love of the land had been bred into her, part of her Irish heritage, and even now, though her body was on fire and her arms and legs covered in scratches from the cane, it was joy to watch the harvesting of the crop and to know she had helped as much as any nineteen-year-old girl could.

Or should be expected to! The whispers of the townspeople cut in on her.

These days O'Mara couldn't care less, drinking steadily so he couldn't think about losing his wife and the son he idolised. Though the images of her mother and brother often passed before Catherine's eyes, she couldn't allow herself the luxury of expressing her grief, for now her father leant on her, as he had on her mother, as a source of strength.

She still cried at night. How could she not? It was only twelve months since Patrick, driving the jeep, with his mother as a passenger, had lost control on the back road and ploughed into a tree. There had been no hiding the fact that Patrick had been driving recklessly, but even to this day O'Mara wouldn't accept it. After all, Patrick had been perfect and if Charles O'Mara had to lose one of his children, it would never have been his son. In those early, terrible days after the tragedy, her father had never tired of telling her. Sons were precious, a man couldn't live without one, but for a daughter he had never had much time.

Later he had turned to her because she had her mother's strength, but the whole world of love in him had been given to Patrick and no one else. On rare occasions, as now, tears filled Catherine's emerald eyes, but she blinked them away fiercely. No one could make her father love her though she would do anything to please him—turn herself into a labourer, a field hand, give up her ambitions to stay home and look after him. She had been an excellent student, far better than Patrick, and it had been her mother's dream to send her on to University.

'Mamma!' Catherine whispered the word aloud, then bit on her lip until she drew blood. She would never see her mother again, except maybe in Heaven, and God knows she couldn't seem to believe in that any more. There was nothing but work and no pay, but at least she had the great natural beauty of the land to lend her strength.

So engrossed was she in her train of thought, she didn't hear the sound of a jeep until it was almost upon her. In the same moment she saw Bert and Mario on the tractor raise their hands and she snapped upright, something in the animated yet respectful greetings alerting her to the identity of the newcomer.

'Catherine?'

He was out of the jeep and moving towards her,

unsmiling, his grim gaze taking in every detail of her unhappiness, confusion and just plain exhaustion.

'Good morning, Mr Hungerford!' she said jauntily, mimicking her father's soft brogue. 'O'Mara isn't home today.'

'I didn't expect it.'

She shrugged a little helplessly at the curt tone. 'Merely district gossip, sir. My father doesn't drink half as much as he's supposed to. He couldn't!'

'But enough!' There was no mistaking the contempt in his eyes. 'Did he by any chance say when he would be back?'

'He could be back already for all I know,' she answered, still in the same false, jaunty tone.

'Co-operative little thing, aren't you?' He narrowed his eyes. 'Hadn't you better get out of the hot sun before that young skin turns to leather?'

'In a little while,' she said, ignoring him. 'I'm admiring the scenery.'

'More likely you're too damned tired to move. Get out.'

'What did you say?' She turned back to him sweetly, her quick temper sparkling in her eyes.

'You heard. *Get out.* I'll drive you back up to the house.'

'I think you mean it,' she said, deliberately needling him though she knew she shouldn't.

'I do!' he returned grimly, staring at the long scratches on her slender legs. 'Making a slave of yourself is becoming too much your way of life.'

'Ah then, but I wasn't brought up with a silver spoon in my mouth.'

'No, just a solid diet of vinegar.'

'Is that how you think of me?'

He was so tall she had to twist her head to look up at him.

'Who said I think of you at all?'

'Of course, it's your social conscience. I've heard of it before. What is it you want anyway?' she asked ironically. 'I can tell you all you need to know.'

'A paragon of virtues!' For an instant there was a flickering light in the depths of his eyes. 'A quick tongue and a lively intelligence—and your mother's beauty under all the dirt and the horrifying scratches.'

'How does one avoid it when you work the cane?' She was stung by his brutality, lifting her hand and further smearing a trail of red dust to the point of her chin.

'This is madness. You know that,' he said in a harsh undertone.

'I think not. I'm young and healthy.'

'And you're the talk of the district. Trying to do a man's work when the breeze could blow you away. Needless to say, everyone admires you like crazy.'

'Except you.'

'I think you're a little fool. How is your father ever going to stand by himself if you won't let him?'

'*Damn* you!' She stared at him, all her antagonisms transmuted to explosive action.

He must have seen the fighting rage in her face, for as she swung up her hand he caught it and nearly swung her off her feet. 'Hate me all you like,' he gritted, 'but don't ever raise your hand to me again, or I might teach you a lesson. Brave you might be, but very easy to punish.'

'I'm sorry.' Catherine tried to twist away, devastated by his strength.

'You're not!' His glance slid over her without gentleness. 'If you want to lie to me you'd better veil your eyes—they're crystal clear and as green as grass. Go and sit in the jeep and wait for me. I want to have a word with the men.'

'It's kind of you,' she retorted, 'but they obey me!'

'Let's say they're doing the job they were born to. Sit in and be quiet.'

'Dictator!'

'That's right.' He studied her for a moment, then he turned and walked away towards the men, who immediately brought their machinery to a halt.

Go on, give the orders! Catherine muttered to herself. *You're the Big Man in these parts.*

Everything about David Hungerford upset her. His manner and appearance. Over six feet, with a superbly sleek and co-ordinated body, he put her in mind of some great golden puma relentlessly stalking its objective. His hair was blue-black, his eyes a clear amber against his golden bronze skin. He was striking beyond question, but about as lovable as the big jungle cat and about as easy to handle.

The Hungerfords had pioneered the North, but sugar was nowdays only a fraction of their interests. They were immensely wealthy and on the death of his father, in a plane crash in New Guinea, David Hungerford had taken over the reins so that Hungerford Holdings had no parallel in the North.

His was a position of responsibility and power, and Catherine couldn't quite believe in his humanitarianism. What was it he really wanted—the farm? It didn't seem likely when he owned vast tracts of land. Of course people persisted in taking their troubles and complaints to him and a lot of people had remarked on O'Mara's decline. As neighbours everyone had been marvellous and very gentle to their grief, but inevitably her father's bitterness and uncertain temper had driven them away. O'Mara had no worse enemy than himself. And Catherine had become a talking point in the district.

When he came back to the jeep she didn't even turn her head and whatever it was he was going to say he dropped. The sun was scorching, a great ball of fire, but still she whipped off her coolie hat so she could feel the breeze through her cloudy masses of hair. She had pinned it haphazardly on top of her head, now it escaped from its few pins to whip into a dark tangle of curls, falling just past her shoulders.

'How you don't have freckles beats me.' He glanced at her fleetingly.

'Surely old leather is enough?'

'You have fabulous skin, as you know, but I'm not sure how long you can maintain it at this rate.'

'Who cares?' She tipped her head back so her hair fell like a waterfall down her back.

'Aren't I to believe the rumours, then?'

'Which ones?' she asked bitterly, falling into the trap.

'Young Morley. Doesn't he head your long list of admirers?'

'You know more about it than I do,' she shrugged.

'I don't want him coming out to the farm when your father's not home.'

'*What?*' she demanded. 'To relieve your vulgar curiosity, I haven't seen him for a week.'

'That's because he's away.'

'I don't mind,' she answered truthfully. Fond as she was of Jon she had no romantic feelings for him whatever. There was no room for romance in her life. It was silly and unpleasant, and when all was said and done it turned a woman into a slave for life.

'Which, alack, isn't Morley's story. Just to see him look at you would make anyone sick.'

'Oh?' she burst out, irrepressibly tart, 'and when were you peering at us both?'

'Plenty of times. I don't blame him. You're beautiful to look at. Just to look at.'

'You surprise me,' she retorted, 'but I'm glad of a little compliment.'

'When you're scrubbed,' he added.

'Yes, I have to admit a shower would be a good idea.' Unabashed. she glanced down at her T-shirt and brief shorts. It was hard to escape the red dust. At the harvesting it rose and choked the throat and nostrils and put a fine film over one's clothes.

'It's a bad time for your father to be out of business,' he said unpleasantly. 'You know as well as I do the cane has to be taken to the mill as quickly as possible. He's risking losing the crop. It will be a write-off after another day.'

'*I'm* trving!' Catherine turned on him emotionally, realising he was speaking the literal truth. The sugar content of cane deteriorated very rapidly, and she had the horrible suspicion O'Mara was working himself up for another binge.

'It's not good enough,' he answered more gently. 'How bad are things at the farm?'

'They're not bad at all,' she said huskily because she was tired. 'Not good, I suppose, but not bad either. O'Mara's had a bad time. I have to be careful not to worry him.'

'And what about you?' he countered curtly. 'Does it really help him to have you there? He's drained your youth and your strength, and I've never yet seen him show you a fraction of the love and the pride he lavished on your brother.'

'Patrick was special,' she said humbly. 'I can never take his place.'

'Your father is the only one who thought so. You've been too much alone.'

The kindness in his voice, the faint tenderness, filled her with an odd kind of panic. Better he was cruel to her.

Better for *what*?

Agitated now, she looked with relief towards the house. It badly needed another paint, for paint blistered in the hot sun, but she was sure they couldn't afford it. If only O'Mara cared!

'Catherine?' David Hungerford pulled the jeep into the shade of the poinciana and turned to look at her.

'Don't ask me questions, *please*!'

'No, it's like to trying to tie down a cat. If you need help you know where to come.'

'I'll try not to bother you.' She was too tired for grace, almost stumbling out of the jeep.

'Don't be too independent, will you?' He caught at her wrist and held her there. 'You can't go it alone and you can't afford to lose the crop.'

'I have Bert and Mario!' It was impossible not to get excited, her green eyes blazing in her small golden-tanned face.

'Who are worried, don't you know?'

For a moment Catherine couldn't speak and the tears stood in her eyes. She hated them, but they were there and he had seen them. 'O'Mara will be back this afternoon.'

'He'd better be, because you can't take any more.' Savagely he backed the jeep up, then swung it towards the gateway spanned by an archway of purple-flowering morning glories. He didn't turn to wave and Catherine didn't think to wave either. What was there to wave about anyway? They were worlds apart in every way.

Wearily she pulled herself up the stairs, considering what best to do after she had had a bite of lunch. She couldn't go into the town, checking on O'Mara. It would anger him dreadfully. Inside the house, she gulped down a glass of milk, ate a sandwich and hurriedly left. Coming back to the house with David Hungerford had only been a token gesture. She could easily have gone without lunch, there was so much to be done.

By the end of the day she was almost reduced to real tears. O'Mara hadn't returned and Bert and Mario had more or less told her they wouldn't be available for very much longer. As usual, they hadn't been paid, but they were too kindhearted to leave her. As Bert put it: 'A fair go's a fair go, but where's your dad?'

At sunset Bert called a halt and Mario dropped her back at the house. 'Your father's not here, then,' he said, staring up at the darkened house.

'No. I've almost given him up.' Fleetingly she smiled into the dark, understanding eyes. 'Go on home, Mario. It looks like a hard day tomorrow.'

'Such a pity!' Mario remarked. 'Your father wasn't the only one to be hurt. Why don't you clear out?'

'I'm staying,' she told him. 'This is my home.'

In the bathroom she stripped off her clothes and got in under the shower, letting it rain down over her head before she began rubbing shampoo into her aching head. Mario's words came back to her and she sighed aloud. How could she clear out? She had nothing, no one, and perhaps this miserable episode in their lives would pass. Tears of pain and frustration scalded her eyes. Perhaps something terrible had happened to her father? She felt so tired, her brain had lost its ability to think clearly, but at least it was something to be really clean again.

Outside the shower cubicle, she was facing a full-length mirror. Usually out of modesty she took little notice of her reflection, but now for no seeming reason she dwelt on the sight of her own naked body.

She was down to a dancer's weight—less. Small, high breasts, tiny waist, narrow hips, slender legs. She had never in her life thought of herself as a woman, and desirable; now her own image seemed wildly erotic. Colour flushed her skin and inside the

curling, raven masses of her hair, her green eyes
looked immense.

Beauty. Was that what David Hungerford saw?
A wild mop of hair, too pronounced bones and a
flawless Irish skin turned gilt by an alien sun. Her
mother's beauty? Not a fraction of it. The features
were the same, the same colouring, but not that exquisitely gentle and dreaming expression. There
was passion in Catherine's face, a desperation that
made her look startlingly different.

She turned away from her oddly bewitching reflection and slipped into her robe. Just a whisper of
green crêpe-de-chine, but that was all she could
bear. The house was so quiet she could hear her
own breathing. It was impossible to eat, she was too
worried, yet she hesitated to take the plunge and
ring around. This wasn't the first time her father
had stayed out all day and into the night and he
wouldn't thank her for her enquiries. Catherine
loved her father, but his escalating problem and the
attendant irresponsibility was a source of great
anxiety to her.

Didn't O'Mara realise she too was bereft?
Though she had had to listen to him sobbing and
ranting against the Almighty, always with the
whisky bottle close at hand, the rare times her
façade had cracked a little he became aggressive and
angry, chiding her for plunging herself into a
morass of self-pity. The thing was, he didn't really
want to know how she felt. It was enough for him
to bear his own pain.

With crystal clarity Catherine saw so many scenes
from the past. Her father with Patrick on his shoul-

ders, teaching him how to swim and shoot and ride, lavishing one small boy with expensive toys, face always smiling, voice full of pride. Patrick had meant everything to her father. Far, far more than she and her mother put together and Patrick had been lovable. Almost always, but his monstrous recklessness had killed her mother. She couldn't bear to think about it.

Shortly after nine, when she heard a car turn into the drive, she ran to the door and opened it up. She had turned the outside lights on long ago and her heart lurched with fright as she recognised David Hungerford's station wagon. She was frightened now, really frightened.

'David?' It was the first time she had ever ventured to call him by his Christian name and he slipped from behind the wheel and looked up at her.

'It's all right.'

For a second she stood in the shadows looking down at him, then she flew down the stairs, guessing the situation.

'It's O'Mara, isn't it?'

'I've brought him home.'

'Oh, bravo!' she cried, and hoped he couldn't hear the sob behind the bitter sarcasm.

'Don't bug me, little one,' he said crisply. 'Though I was fairly sure of your reaction.'

Without even glancing at her he walked around to the passenger seat of the car and opened it out.

'Is he unconscious, then?' Catherine demanded, shocked at how angry she was when he had really come to her rescue.

'Dead drunk,' he returned, too damn pat.

'It happens,' she said loyally.

'In your father's case, a lot.'

It was a good thing he was so strong, because he had to hoist O'Mara over his shoulder, his hard, handsome face completely expressionless. 'Come on, Catherine, co-operate. We'd better put him to bed.'

She didn't understand how she felt, but she wasn't going to thank him. 'You'd better follow me, then.'

'Thanks,' he returned dryly. 'You're a funny little creature.'

Silently Catherine ran ahead of him, switching on lights as she went. Hang the electricity bill. In her father's room she turned back the quilt with trembling hands, humiliation burning inside her like acid.

'Put him down,' she said flatly.

'I'd be pleased to,' he returned and deposited the dead weight of his heavy burden on the bed.

'Oh, O'Mara!' Catherine bit on her lip before floods of emotion overcame her. 'You didn't deserve this.'

Even dead drunk with his mouth slightly open, her father was a handsome man—black Irish with a hard tan and the long mobile mouth slack. In the old days, though he had always liked to pass his time in the pub he had been charming and gregarious and he had always come home straight afterwards. Now he was putting his very life in danger.

'Leave him to me.' David Hungerford got a grip on her shoulders and put her away from the bed.

'Do you really think I'm not capable of attending

to my own father?' Perversely she was transferring her furies to him.

'Just try and keep calm.' The coldness in his voice had the sting of a whip. 'If you want to make yourself useful, go and make some coffee.'

'For O'Mara?' Startled she swallowed the sob in her throat.

'For me!' he corrected her with a flickering amber glance. 'O'Mara can sleep it off.'

When he came into the kitchen he stood leaning against the doorway watching her while she set out their best coffee cups and saucers. It was a dreadful effort to say something, but it had to be said.

'Thank you, Mr Hungerford,' she said tersely, turning her head slightly so he couldn't see the helpless rage in her eyes. 'It won't happen again.'

'I thought *David* was too much to hope for!' He bowed slightly from the waist and it looked incredibly elegant. 'For your sake, Catherine, far more than your father's, I hope not. He's been drinking recklessly for more than a year now and always under stress. A lot of people are concerned about him.'

'O'Mara doesn't give a damn for anyone!' she exclaimed loyally.

'I can see that.'

'Can you now?' Her eyes flashed, so big and so green they dominated her small golden face. 'Don't let gossip convince you my father doesn't care about me—he *does*.'

'Don't get violent, Catherine,' he said calmly.

'You unnerve me. I don't suppose we like each other. Anyway, what's it to be, black or white?'

'Black.' He started away from the door, immediately reducing the dimensions of the room, and before Catherine could help herself she took a few little steps backwards in involuntary retreat.

'What the devil's the matter now?' he demanded.

'You frightened me. You have a way of moving. . . .' For the life of her she couldn't smile or tell him about her fanciful notion of a golden puma.

'You've got to be kidding!' He wasn't smiling either, and his sardonic voice seemed full of a contemptuous pity.

'No, I'm not kidding. Not at all.'

'I couldn't bear to hear what's going on in that schoolgirl mind,' he said cruelly.

'Nothing like that.' Colour whipped under her skin.

'Let's hope not. You're a lot safer with me than those youngsters you hang around with. Especially if you greet them in a whisper of green silk.' His eyes skimmed her lightly but with such effrontery she nearly choked.

'I feel sure you know what a woman looks like,' she said crossly.

'Perhaps. Anyway, it suits you. I don't think for a moment, Catherine, you're trying to be consciously provocative.'

'Be sure of it,' she returned tartly. 'I'd just as soon charm a puma.'

'Is that some kind of an allusion to me?' he asked, narrow-eyed.

'I expect it is. You're very sleek.' Hate was stirring in her—hate and something unfamiliar. 'If you'll give me a minute, I'll dress.'

'Don't bother. I'm not a cradle robber.'

But which way was he looking at her? For all her antipathy she felt as if she was melting inside. Disturbed, Catherine crossed to the stove, where the coffee was gently perking. She wasn't wearing anything on her feet either, and she realised she wouldn't even come up to his shoulder.

'Come along, Catherine,' he was somewhere behind her, coaxing her with a mixture of amusement and impatience. 'I won't do or say a thing to make you nervous. Not tonight at any rate!'

A tremor ran like a ripple over Catherine's entire body and her hand trembled so violently the coffee splashed out of the spout and down over her left hand. 'Ouch!' she exclaimed.

In an instant he was beside her, taking the coffee pot out of her nerveless fingers and drawing her forcibly to the sink. 'If I'd known I was going to rattle you so much, I'd never have asked for the goddamn coffee!'

'It's nothing!' For a minute or two she was afraid of her own senses, so close to him, while he held her hand firmly under the cold running tap.

'You're the bravest little kid I ever saw!' His sculptured mouth thinned and he grabbed a clean tea-towel and patted her hand dry. 'Hands like these shouldn't have callouses on the palms.'

'I don't need you to admire me.' Her whole body was trembling now with barely concealed emotion.

'Make up your mind,' he said curtly.

Everything was coming adrift. Her whole life. She seemed to be frozen, unable to move, while he towered over her, searching her brilliant eyes. If there was any pain in her hand she couldn't feel it, for the violent turbulence in her blood.

'Why don't you just leave?' she said bitterly.

'Why not?' The words slashed at her. 'You're acting like a childish little idiot. Do you really think I'm going to flip because you've grown into a beauty and you're just barely covered?'

'You brute!' she hissed painfully. 'Go away!'

'And let you cry your eyes out?'

'I haven't cried for a long time.'

'So maybe you need the relief. If you take so much on, you're bound to suffer.'

She knew it was true and she let out a gasp, then a stifled sob. 'I should be grateful to you, but I'm not!'

'I know that. Shall I tell you why?' He stared at her with his gleaming eyes.

Catherine didn't answer—couldn't. She knew if she said a word it would whirl her into danger. Nothing had prepared her for the deep and quivering sensations in her own body, primeval sensations that shocked and shamed her.

'Catherine?'

He had a very attractive voice, deep and resonant, and she made a little sound of pain, swinging her head away so the dark cloud of her hair fell away from her exquisitely boned face.

'I don't like you, Mr Hungerford. I thought you knew that.'

'You've got a crazy way of trying to convince me.' He gave a short laugh.

To her horror, her eyes filled with tears and she shook her head back and forth, humiliated, excited and frightened. Was she so obvious in showing her reactions?

'Let's have that coffee,' he said flatly. 'I guess you haven't bothered eating today?'

'There were a hundred and one things to attend to,' she answered just as shortly. 'Don't worry about me, Mr Hungerford, I don't need your pity.'

'You'll get turned over my knee if you keep up that tone,' he promised dryly. 'After all, your circumstances being what they are, I'd have to feel some concern for you.'

'Thank you.' Nothing would make her look at him, meet the extraordinary intensity of his gaze.

He pulled out a chair for her and she sat down, drawing the lapels of her robe together. It was a fact that she was adequately covered, yet she felt deeply embarrassed every time his eyes fell on her.

'What about some toast?' he said, with a purposeful air.

'Very well.' She thought she detected amusement in his eyes.

'I'll get it.' His expression changed and he moved away from her, going to the bread crock and removing half a loaf of bread. 'Tell me, are you sleeping?' he asked casually.

'Yes.' She was instantly on guard.

'Discourteous child.' Within seconds he had the bread in the toaster and was now at the refrigerator.

'So have a laugh about that!' Catherine pulled herself up, humiliation flaring through her whole body.

'I'm not laughing.' He made one move to restrain her, holding her by the shoulder. The refrigerator was almost pitifully empty and oh, how she wished he had never opened it. She was so confused and so tired.

'Doesn't your father give you any money at all?' he asked bluntly.

'Of course he does!' Her feelings were sharply etched in her small face. 'I just haven't done the shopping, that's all. I haven't had time to get in an order.'

'Then you'll ring Collins in the morning and tell him exactly what you want.'

'And who'll pay?' she flashed back at him, and coloured deeply at her own admission.

'I will,' he said harshly. 'Do you think I'm going to stand around and watch you starve?'

'I should think you'd enjoy it.'

'My God!' With his strong hands he seized her and Catherine knew a moment of great fear, beyond anything she had ever felt in her whole life. He looked as if he wanted to beat her, for there was passion and ruthlessness in his face.

'I'm sorry.' The fright stood in her face and her green eyes. 'I didn't mean that.'

'Don't tempt me again.' Suddenly he released her so that she almost reeled. 'You like to lash out with your little insults, but you might as well know you're no longer safe from reprisals.'

She fell silent then and after a moment he took butter and cheese from the refrigerator and set it down on the table, staring at her with his brilliant amber eyes.

'I'm not asking you to put your pride in your pocket, just accept a little help from a neighbour.

Afterwards you can pay me back.'

'My father gives me everything he can,' she whispered, and slumped down at the table, defeated.

'Everything he can spare from the drink. Don't lie to me, Catherine.'

'It's my life,' she protested.

'Really? I thought it was suicide.' Rather violently he shoved a sandwich towards her. 'Eat up.'

'I can't. I feel wretched.'

'You can.' He spoke quietly, but with deadly seriousness.

'All right.' It was easy to submit. 'Are you having anything yourself?'

'I'm not hungry.' He waited while she ate the sandwich, then he made her another. 'What does the farm mean to you anyway?'

'My life.'

'Except within a year you'll probably be married.'

'Never.' It was pure reaction.

'Then perhaps you'll be kind enough to tell young Morley.'

'Jon?' She lifted her head briefly.

'Didn't you know he's madly in love with you?'

'How tiresome. Anyway, his mother doesn't think I'm half good enough for him.'

'Dear me, you're quite a favourite of mine.'

'I understand a joke.'

'No joke,' he said dryly, and put milk in her coffee. 'Are you trying to tell me you have no feeling for Morley at all?'

'I adore him. What I don't understand is why you want an answer.'

'Well, Jon does work for me,' he said leaning back in his chair.

'And it's you that sends him travelling?'

'Of course. I can't have you settling for young Morley. That would be a tragedy.'

'We used to be great friends when we were children,' she said.

'Such a long time ago.' He was watching her small face intently. 'He was your brother's best friend, wasn't he?'

'Oh yes,' her green eyes were sad and dreamy, remembering. 'O'Mara allowed it because Jon was such a good influence on Patrick. You know how he is, Jon doesn't like trouble. I was the one who was always getting Patrick into scrapes, or so O'Mara convinced me. He's never forgiven me for being the one to survive.'

'Though you'd make two of your father and brother.'

'How can you say that?' she cried in a stricken voice. 'It's killing O'Mara that he'll never see Patrick again.'

'Doesn't your church assure him he will?'

'I don't know. I don't know if it's true,' she said with quiet desperation. 'This year has changed me.'

'You've been working too hard, and it can't go on. I won't have it. The town won't have it. Many people have tried to help your father, but he's grown very bitter, abrasive.'

'Don't hold it against him,' Catherine begged in a soft voice. 'I swear he'll come out of it.'

'In the meantime, he's going to make *you* do penance—nurturing, slaving, comforting with very little comfort yourself. What's going to happen about the harvesting?'

'I'll have him up in the morning.' She willed spirit into her soft, husky voice. 'No one can work better than O'Mara when he's well.'

'You know if you need help, where to come?' He reached over and caught her by the wrist.

'That would be precipitating a crisis,' she said uneasily. 'O'Mara never asks for help.'

'I'm not interested in O'Mara,' he said harshly, and stood up. 'I'm afraid you'll injure or even kill yourself. That tractor isn't very safe.'

'It's the best we can do. Anyway, Mario's been managing it for a long time.'

'Then your help won't be needed. It's nearly midnight. Time you went to bed.'

'This time next year, perhaps it will all seem like a bad dream.' She stood up to join him, very small by his shoulder.

'Give me your solemn promise you'll ring Collins in the morning.'

'A nice thought, but I can't do it. O'Mara would wonder where it all came from.'

'Tell him Jim let you book it up until after the harvest.'

'And what do I tell Jim?' She lifted her dazed eyes to his arrogant, sculptured head.

'Don't concern yourself with that. I'll speak to him and explain it's only by way of a loan. Order what you need each week and you can clear the bill with me when you're ready.'

His amber eyes touched her face briefly, then they were moving out on to the verandah. The stars were glistening with great beauty, diamonds upon velvet, and she who loved order and beauty gave a deep sigh.

'Thank you for bringing O'Mara home. If I've said anything to offend you, I'm sorry. I'm still confused by what's been happening around here since my mother and Patrick died.'

He turned back to look at her, a measure of pity in his gleaming eyes. 'You're young, Catherine. Try and rejoice in it and not dwell on the past. I know your pain, more than you can be expected to bear, but you have your mother's strength and in you her beauty endures. You'll make it, but you're still young enough to need a little help.'

Her head ached as she rested it against the vine-wreathed timber support, watching while his headlights flared into life, then the big station wagon pulled away.

In his bedroom O'Mara was sleeping deeply, a flush across his darkened skin. Catherine stood for a moment looking down at him, then with tears in her eyes she turned away, switching off the lamp that had lent a softening glow to the small room. Patrick's room. Her father had slept here ever since that dreadful day. In Patrick he had found his immortality; now with Patrick gone he cared nothing for life. No matter what she did, no matter how she cared, she couldn't share in her father's life, but she couldn't leave him in his present state. He knew that, just as she knew it, for she was much, much older than her actual years.

When she turned the lamp out in her own room

she was asleep almost at once, only to dream herself in the jungle, a gazelle stalked by a great cat who looked out upon his world with David Hungerford's burnished eyes.

CHAPTER TWO

O'MARA woke in the morning in a fine temper and bellowed from the bedroom for his breakfast. Ten minutes later he joined Catherine in the kitchen, his headache and the sickness inside him showing in his bloodshot blue eyes and hangdog expression.

'What's this, then?' He sat down heavily at the table, staring at the plate of bacon, eggs and tomato as though he couldn't believe it.

'Mr Collins brought the order first thing this morning,' Catherine answered, her heart beating fast.

'And how the devil are we going to pay him? Just tell me that?'

'He's prepared to wait.' Catherine always answered her father in a curiously soft soothing voice.

'And wait he will!' O'Mara gave a harsh laugh that shut off abruptly. 'You wouldn't be lying to me, girl?'

'Jim is very definitely prepared to wait until after the harvest.'

'Well now, and who do we have to thank for that?' O'Mara swept out his arm and grasped his daughter by the wrist. 'It wouldn't have anything to do with Hungerford, would it now?'

'How could you think that?' It took courage to meet the bitter blue gaze.

'Because he's rich and we're poor,' said O'Mara, sighing despairingly. 'He must have a low opinion of me.'

'No.' Catherine moved forward compassionately and bowed her chin on her father's fine head. 'You're the most important person in the world.'

'No, Kate.' O'Mara sighed again. 'Say anything you like to me—I don't deserve you, I know.'

So rare was the note of caring, Catherine didn't know whether to laugh or to cry, but she knew she couldn't dally in case O'Mara's mood changed. 'I wish you'd eat up your breakfast, it's going cold,' she said gently and patted her father's shoulder. 'Bert and Mario will be pleased to see you.'

'Perhaps.' O'Mara smiled a little drearily. 'Sometimes I wonder, Katie, if it's worth surviving. My son gone, my wife. Well, there's the farm, all I have. It's yours.'

'And what would anything matter without you?' Catherine said roughly, wounded all over again by the sad and lonely expression. 'It's been bad, O'Mara, bad for both of us, but you can't turn your back on the world. Build a new one.'

'Aw, for God's sake!' O'Mara shoved his plate away and stood up. 'Isn't that too easy for a little girl? If I choose to turn my back on the world, or better yet, drink myself to death, that's my business. Nobody loved Patrick like I did. He alone made me happy. You understand?' His voice boomed,

trembled, accused, and Catherine shut her eyes and
turned away to the sink.

'If I could bring Patrick back to you, O'Mara, I
would,' she sighed.

'And I would let you go,' O'Mara cried passionately, his face flushing so he looked ill and distraught. 'I know you're a good girl, but you're not
important, that's all.'

The back door banged and after a minute Catherine heard the utility start up. She still stood at the
sink, her heart and hands cold, inside weeping, but
outside under control. Strong men didn't die of a
broken heart and it had only been a year. Eventually time would ease the pain and O'Mara would
begin to recover. He was still in his prime. Time
enough to father a brood of sons, now Patrick was
gone.

Turning, she noticed her father had barely
touched the food on his plate, but at least he had
accepted her haunted little lie. Obviously David
Hungerford had considered she wouldn't accept
his offer by morning, so he had contacted Jim
Collins himself. Jim had arrived just before seven,
cheerful and matter-of-fact, happy to be of service
and anxious to put her at her ease. Jim was a good,
decent person, like most of the town.

When she arrived at the canefields thirty minutes
later, her father's unhappy passion had exploded
into a wild anger. He was standing over the short,
stocky Mario bellowing that this was *his* domain, his
farm, and he had better have a care how he talked.

'What is it?' Catherine ran forward quickly,
ashamed at the way Mario was being bombarded. It

was so unfair when Mario had given of his very best for years and even now hadn't been paid for weeks. 'Can I help?' she repeated, frightened by the way her father's personality had changed.

'Stay away!' O'Mara turned on her a violent face. 'You surely don't own the farm yet!'

The look of contempt that passed across Mario's swarthy face was so transparent it provoked O'Mara into nearly jerking him off his feet.

'For God's sake, O'Mara, let him go!' Catherine grabbed her father's arm tensely and the next minute found herself sprawling as her father flung back his arm in reaction.

'I told you, Katie, keep out of this!'

Catherine sat there in the rubble almost paralysed then she sprang to her feet again, crying out again in as sharp a voice as she could muster, 'Doesn't it matter to you, then, that Mario has worked for us for years? Doesn't it matter that we need him and he's been working without pay for at least three weeks?'

'It doesn't give him the right to judge me or my way of life!' O'Mara moved his head to meet his daughter's brilliant gaze. 'Please tell him he's dismissed. I'll get a cheque to him as quickly as possible.'

'But we *need* him!' Catherine pleaded, but her father had turned away, a dark brooding figure, his eyes on the harvester in the distance.

'It's all right,' Mario said to Catherine rather brusquely. 'Your father is a changed man—too excitable, too angry. It will help if I go away for a while.'

'But what did you say to him?' Catherine looked into Mario's dark eyes, noticing for the first time that the man was trembling. 'Oh, I'm so sorry, Mario. More sorry than I can say.'

'I know that.' Gently he put his hand on her shoulder. 'Don't young girls want to be happy, enjoy life? You must get away from this place. Your father is never going to change.'

'You can't be sure of that, Mario. I can't just give up on him.'

'Then I can only hope that things turn out for you. No one could have been sweeter or kinder to me than your dear mamma, and what I have done I've done for her sake—and yours. Someone had to speak to your father and if he's cursing me now, some little grains of truth may sink in. You've been working too hard for too long, a little slip of a girl. Valeria told me to speak out and I did. She won't mind that your father has dismissed me. I can find work almost immediately.'

'But we can't find a worker such as you!' Catherine answered directly. 'Tell me, Mario, what am I to do?'

Mario compressed his full lips, his expression troubled. 'If you don't get the harvest in, you're ruined.'

'But there's no one to help us. No one who can handle the machinery like you.'

'Your father should have thought of that before he tried to crush me with his bare hands!' Mario exclaimed with faint humour. 'He's very strong, you know. Immensely to a little man like me. Let him do it on his own.'

'He surely won't speak to Bert?' Catherine looked out nervously at the fields.

'Ah, Bert,' Mario adjusted his hat thoughtfully. 'Bert has proved his worth a hundred times over and he's so quiet he's never in any kind of trouble. Bert will stay.'

'Thank God!' Catherine gave a profound sigh of relief. 'Perhaps this will blow over in a day or two.'

'No matter!' Mario threw up his hands in a volatile gesture. 'I'm sorry for you, little one, but I will never work for your father again. I can't. Others have lost sons, wives, lovers. Life deals out many blows, and in times of stress one must go to God. It is bad for a man to live with despair in his heart. And there's you. Few men would allow their daughters to work so hard.'

'I'm strong.' Catherine didn't move. Even when Mario patted her shoulder and moved away.

And now what were they to do?

By late afternoon, the ancient tractor had ground to a stop, and O'Mara, never handy with his hands, stood over it swearing terribly.

'How bad is it?' Catherine asked, as Bert seemed unable to speak.

'Bloody jammed!' O'Mara made a gesture of intense exasperation and despair and blood spurted from his hand. 'There's a trick in it, I suppose, but only that idiot Mario can handle it.'

'Will I get him?'

'You will *not*!' O'Mara roared, and wrapped a none too clean handkerchief around his mildly injured hand. 'I'd rather call your boy-friend.'

'Jon?' Catherine looked her astonishment and even Bert flashed a look of scorn.

'Hungerford!' O'Mara bit off grimly.

'How absolutely extraordinary!' Catherine looked bemused by the very idea.

'I wonder!' O'Mara picked up a tool and threw it down again in disgust. 'Is it possible, Albert, you haven't learned anything in all these years? How do you get the bloody thing to go?'

'Ya brought it all on yaself, O'Mara, sacking Mario.' Bert gave vent to his resentments, his laconic voice full of a new disapproval.

'And I'll sack you too, come to that!'

'It's orright with me.'

'Are you all going mad?' Catherine was almost dancing in her frustration. 'You're fighting among yourselves and we're facing ruin!'

'On the other hand, who cares?' O'Mara said wearily.

'Please, Bert!' Catherine fixed the unhappy Bert with a pleading eye, but under it there was iron.

'I won't let ya down, Miss Cathy, but as ya dad says, how do we get the bloody thing to go? It wouldn't be easy to borrow another one either. O'Mara's complicated things with his rages and it's a busy time for everyone. Mario's the mechanical genius.'

'Compared to you I suppose so!' O'Mara's head was throbbing dreadfully, yet he gave a wry laugh. Mario's ability with machinery was slightly better than rudimentary.

'Oh dear, dear, dear!' For a minute only Catherine buried her face in her hands, then invariably she burst out with a solution. 'I'd better run for the nearest help.'

'Hungerford?' O'Mara roared, glaring at his daughter indignantly.

'Ya shoulda thought of that earlier,' Bert told her, his long face brightening considerably. 'Now Mr Hungerford, he *is* a genius. An engineer an' all!'

'Hah!' O'Mara grunted. 'Infallible!'

'Are you going to let me go, O'Mara?' Catherine looked directly at her father.

'No, I most definitely am *not*!'

'Aren't ya?' Bert looked surprised. 'What about goin' yaself, then?'

'You don't leave me much choice.' O'Mara threw up his hands, almost desperate for a drink. 'If there's one thing that gets me down it's having to beg for anything.'

'But we're only asking for a little help with our machine!' Catherine dragged herself off the ancient tractor.

'Damn and blast!' O'Mara shook his head, looking disgruntled. 'At least he won't be surprised.'

Catherine waited for no further answer, but tore away to the old utility. It was more than likely David Hungerford wouldn't be at home, but she could leave a message. He was the only hope they had. If he couldn't fix the tractor himself, surely he could come up with someone. It meant pocketing her pride, but she'd be damned if she was going to let the crop go to ruin.

Fifteen minutes later she was rattling up the long road that cut through the Hungerford plantation and led directly to the house. Here the harvest was almost over and workers, recognising her, waved a cheery greeting, probably wondering what she was doing there. The O'Maras were not and were never likely to be in the Hungerfords' exclusive circle and Catherine, like most of the ordinary folk, was only familiar with the house from a distance.

Today, as always, it looked beautiful, a mansion in the Spanish manner surrounded by wonderful gardens. She passed through the great wrought iron gates that stood open and only then lost her courage. O'Mara was right: it was the hardest thing in the world to go begging, and she was moving into an alien world.

Columns that supported the series of broad arches were wreathed in the magnificent Mexican Blood trumpet vine and she gently touched a blossom before she was plunged from brilliant sunshine into the coolest green shade of the terrace. The ornately carved brass-studded double doors stood open in welcome and for a moment she stared into the high vaulted interior, dazzled by a luxury she had never seen in her life. It was a splendid environment and it suited David Hungerford extraordinarily well. In another minute she would creep away.

'Yes, Missy?'

The voice startled her, the more so because she couldn't see anybody, then a Chinese manservant walked out of the quiet shadows towards her.

'Yes?' he asked again, as though he never in his life expected to see such a dishevelled young woman on his master's doorstep.

'Would Mr Hungerford be at home?' Catherine

asked in her clear, pretty voice, feeling terribly
nervous.

'Yes, missy. May I say who is calling?'

'Catherine O'Mara.' Just a nobody. Belatedly
Catherine considered her appearance through the
servant's eyes. She was in her usual gear of T-shirt
and shorts and she guessed quite correctly that she
didn't pass muster. 'Oh, I won't come in,' she shook
her head, taken back as the man bowed and in-
dicated with his hand that she was to come in and
wait. 'I'm in my working clothes, as you see.'

The Chinese man bowed again and this time there
was a faint smile in his eyes. 'Mr. Hungerford is on
the rear terrace.'

'Then I'll just go round, shall I?' Feeling a perfect fool, Catherine dashed away, racing around
the side of the house to the broad tiled terrace set
with tables and chairs and a swimming pool area
surrounded by abundant tropical planting. There
she came to an abrupt stop.

David Hungerford, looking distinctly unap-
proachable in his impeccable business clothes, was
entertaining a small group of the élite and they all
turned to stare at her as though she had fired a
volley of shots over their beautifully groomed heads.

One of the party was Christina Kimball, a wealthy
farmer nearby, and she recovered first, turning her
blonde head to look at Catherine with an air of
amusement and good-natured contempt.

'Why, it's the little O'Mara girl, isn't it?'

'Catherine?' David Hungerford put his glass
down and came slowly towards her.

'Forgive me, I didn't know you had visitors.' Already Catherine was backing away, lifting her hand to her tangled hair to hold it back.

'That's all right.'

'No, really. . . .' The colour had risen to her cheeks and she was all eyes. 'It's not important.'

'Do bring her over,' Christine drawled. 'We won't bite you, dear.' She glanced at the young man beside her, who laughed loudly.

'It's not important.' Catherine decided this was no time to ask him a favour.

'Let me decide that.' He was close to her and she couldn't breathe because he looked so striking, a little amused by her abruptness, his gleaming eyes seeing the anxiety in her small, flushed face. 'What is it, Catherine? Surely you haven't come all this way to go home again?'

'As it happened, I was just passing,' she informed him abruptly.

'Dave!' Christine called, looking hard at the pair of them.

'Perhaps you could spare me a minute later?' Catherine said quickly and with a faint trace of bitterness.

He answered by turning his head briefly towards the group seated around the marble-topped table and in that instant, Catherine hurried away.

She went like the wind, slamming the door of the utility truck behind her and flying into an unreasonable temper. Damn David Hungerford! Damn the lot of them. The whole district knew Christina Kimball was madly in love with him, and she would make a corker of a wife.

Reversing, she almost clipped David Hungerford's new car, a Jaguar XJS, and that started her off laughing in a peculiar kind of way. If she was going to come up to the house looking like a field hand what did she expect? At least she had given Christine a few moments of malicious amusement. She could even hear her telling her rich friends—'The funniest thing I've seen in years!'

She was off the plantation before she realised there was a car coming up very fast in her rear vision —the Jag. She could scarcely make a run for it when the utility was positively flat out doing fifty. In a wild kind of mutiny she wished she were at the wheel of a high-powered car. She'd give him a run for his money and very likely wrap herself round the nearest tree.

The Jag passed her, ran on a bit further and pulled up. For an instant she considered going right on by, but not only was David Hungerford capable of coming after her, but she desperately needed his help.

Another minute and he half dragged her out of the over-heating utility. 'It's time you and I had a little talk.'

'I'll bet your friends are put out!'

'I don't think *you* have to worry about that.'

Her green eyes were startlingly beautiful, huge and troubled, and some of the tautness died out of his expression. 'Is it your father?' he asked.

'It's the tractor.' Despite herself she couldn't help admiring the elegant perfection of his clothes.

'Broken down?'

'Would I be here if it was still running?' she

said sharply. 'If we don't move we'll never get the cane to the mill!'

'So you need me for what?' he answered just as tartly, sparks of anger in his golden eyes.

'Please, you told me to come to you for help!'

'So I did.' He put out his hand and brushed a streak of dust from her face.

'There's another thing,' she added, 'O'Mara sacked Mario.'

'It sounds like O'Mara,' he answered dryly. 'I suppose in a couple of hours he'll sack Bert.'

'Oh, please, David....' To her horror her voice quavered.

'I might if you promise me something,' he looked down at her with a degree of calculation in his gleaming eyes. 'Just keep calling me David. You're not a schoolgirl any longer tossing a single plait.'

'I promise!' She caught her breath, astounded he could even remember how she had worn her hair.

'All right, stop all this nonsense and go home. I'll be there just as soon as I'm able. You won't be able to do a thing tonight.'

'Thank you!' The weight of her sigh almost buckled her at the knees and he took a step forward, lifting her chin.

'None of this is a major catastrophe, Catherine. If the tractor's had it I'll have to get you another one, that's all.'

'I'm horribly upset about Mario.' She seemed to be swaying, almost falling into his arms, and he wrapped an arm around her tightly and walked her back to his car. 'Hop in.'

'But the utility ... your guests?'

'More than anything I want to get you home. I'll bring the utility back later. I'm sure it's dangerous for you to be driving when you're too tired to stand up.'

'It's the heat! It's been terribly sultry today.'

It was impossible to feel at home in the passenger seat of one of the finest cars in the world. More so dressed the way she was, with the humid heat making her heavy hair curl in a riot around her small, high-boned face. She wanted a shower more than anything else; she felt sticky with the heat and a far cry from the haughty blonde beauty that was still waiting for David at the house.

Inside the car it was absolutely silent. She couldn't even hear the engine running, then he turned a knob and the air-conditioning sprang to life, running at full blast until it cooled the car's interior to the required temperature. Heaven!

'Relax,' he said dryly, with an ironic tenderness beneath.

'Please don't worry about me.'

'Somehow that's a little difficult. You were born to ornament a rich man's home, not run around in that outrageous get-up.'

'Where I come from I'd look silly in a silk dress!' Christine had worn a silk dress, an immaculate white with the soft gleam of gold at her ears and her throat.

'Why so bristly towards Christine?' He glanced at her briefly, a flickering light in his burnished eyes.

'Why, whoever said anything about Miss Kimball?'

'That was a little dig nevertheless.'

'So you *are* going to marry her?'

'I'll have to marry some time!' he laughed softly.

'She's stunning. I'm very pleased for you.'

'Thank you, you little brat.' He glanced her way, but she avoided his eyes. 'The fact is, Catherine, so you won't run away spreading rumours, I admire Christine, but I'm not longing to be trapped.'

'Trapped—*you*?' It burst out of her involuntarily. 'How could anyone dare to trap a cat-man?'

'What the devil is that supposed to mean?' Obviously her remark had arrested him, for the car slowed.

'Oh, an idiotic fancy of mine. You have very unusual eyes and a dangerous way of moving.'

'And it frightens you?'

'Shouldn't it?' She looked at him unsmilingly.

'I told you, didn't I, Catherine, I leave little girls alone.'

'Oh, forget it!' she said feebly. 'I want to thank you anyway for sending Mr Collins round.'

'That's all right, little one,' he said gravely. 'I thought you'd sooner die than take advantage of a little help. Did your father make you suffer for it?'

'What sort of a silly question is that?' Automatically she fired. 'My father worships the ground I walk upon.'

'In any event he didn't notice?'

'No. Mr Collins came early and I hid it all away.'

David just nodded and kept his eye on the road. 'How are you going to manage without Mario?'

'I can drive the tractor.'

'Out of the question.'

'Then I can do all the running back and forth.'

'You're a remarkably spunky little girl,' he returned crisply, 'but I'm not fond of seeing women work out in the fields.'

'Maybe it's my destiny,' she shrugged.

'No.' For an instant his eyes flashed at her, alive with humour and arrogance, and a dangerous sensuality. 'Someone will come along to rescue you.'

'I know him.'

'Really?' he asked bluntly. 'Not your adolescent boy-friend?'

'You're horrid,' she said crossly. 'A sarcastic beast.'

'But you don't know me.'

'I don't want to!' She held herself rigidly in the deep leather seat.

'Well, that's fine.' He stopped abruptly a few yards from the entrance to the farm. 'Get out, Catherine.'

She got out without another word and as soon as she was clear of the car he did a U-turn and took off fast with the red dust from the track settling on the silver paintwork of the car. It was already too late to say she was sorry and he was every bit as dangerous as she had always imagined him to be. She even blushed to remember she once had a crush on him at the age of fourteen. She had won one of the Hungerford scholarships to an excellent private school and he had presented the prizes to a shy but thrilled line-up. Even then she had known a man like that she could never have, but for a long time afterwards the harm was done.

Silly, so silly, he had always produced in her mixed feelings.

When she reached the house, her father gripped her arm so hard she cried out.

'Where the devil have you been?' he demanded.

'What time is it anyway?' She tilted her chin and pulled away.

'Now look here, Katie, don't you start talking to your father like that.' O'Mara sounded quite surprised.

'I'm sorry.' Catherine laughed a little as she said it. 'I've been as quick as I could. He's got visitors, but he's coming back.'

'Thank God!' O'Mara thrust his hands deep into his pockets. 'Bert got me so mad I sent him home. Not that there was anything to do anyway. It's been everyone's day to have a crack at me.'

An hour later David Hungerford returned, and O'Mara, putting on a show of gratitude, took him out to the shed. Catherine had caught the sardonic glint in David Hungerford's eyes, but he had gone quietly saying something to make O'Mara laugh before they were out of earshot. Catherine made no attempt to join them. O'Mara had already warned her off. This was men's work apparently, though she could play the boy for the entire day.

Somehow she had found the time to tidy the house and put fresh flowers in the hallway and on the dining room table. Her mother had always had flowers in the house and Catherine had inherited her gift for arrangement. Now her eye rested on a big copper bowl full of giant cactus dahlias. Yellow was one of her favourite colours, and there was no doubt they lent an extraordinarily decorative touch to the gleaming mahogany table. The dining room suite and one or two pieces of rather beautiful old furniture had come from her mother's old family home and had Catherine known more about antiques, she would have realised they were valuable. As it was, she derived most of her pleasure out of the fact that they had belonged to her mother.

With the men out of the house, she took the opportunity to have a quick shower and change. Though Christine Kimball would never be stuck with nothing to wear, Catherine had a very limited wardrobe indeed. It was a fact that her mother had taught her to sew well, but one still needed money to buy material. As it was she changed into a brightly patterned full skirt in deep peacock colours and added a skimp of a crocheted top she had made herself. She was sick of David Hungerford's cracks about her 'outrageous' gear, so it gave her some satisfaction to notice she looked well in a skirt and top. She would even make herself another skirt the instant she found the time and the money.

It was already dark, for the tropics had no twilight, and Catherine began to wonder if she should ask David Hungerford to share the evening meal with them. It would be the ordinary thing to do with almost anyone else, but of course he was far from ordinary and probably wouldn't rate her invitation very high. She even wondered whether O'Mara would ask him. In the old days O'Mara had been hard to beat for charm when it suited him, which made it all the more difficult to accept his personality change. If only Patrick had lived! Much as she loved her father, she had long since come to the conclusion that O'Mara had never deserved her mother. When he had wanted to tease her, he had called her 'Lady Moira', and although both Patrick and Catherine realised their mother had had a far different background from their father, she rarely spoke of the past. O'Mara hadn't even contacted her family in Ireland after she had died and though Catherine thought of it often, she hadn't the faintest idea who to write to. This was the New World, and very far away.

The roar of the tractor brought her out of her reverie and her heart lifted at the sound. If only O'Mara had known how to do that, she wouldn't be sitting here now wondering how best to thank a man who made her feel beautiful and scruffy and clever and stupid all at the same time.

'It's all right, then!' O'Mara called out to her, as both men approached the verandah. 'Mr Hungerford here has fixed the blessed thing.'

'Wonderful!' Catherine smiled brightly, buoyed up immensely by the ease in O'Mara's face.

'You'll stay to tea, of course?' O'Mara gave the younger man a winning smile. 'Nothing fancy, but my daughter prepares a decent meal, don't you Kate?'

'Perhaps Mr Hungerford....'

'I'd like to.' David Hungerford just looked at her, saving her from rattling on.

'Fine.' For a small time at least O'Mara seemed to have emerged from black despair. 'If you'll come with me now, I'll show you where to wash up.'

Catherine, in shock, kept the smile fixed on her face until both men turned away, then she literally sprang into action, making a dash for the kitchen, her mind frantically considering what she could dish up. There were avocados from the garden for a first course, cheese and fruit for the end, but what for the main course? O'Mara had lost so much interest in food she had settled for a salad and cold meat, but that would never do for a man who had an Italian chef.

Finally, because there wasn't time to deliberate, she settled on avocado, tomato and onion appetiser with a vinaigrette dressing, deep-fried chicken pieces served with the grilled bananas her father liked, herbed and buttered tiny new potatoes, and the delicate flavour of the small green zucchinis Mario had brought her over with a dash of butter, garlic and parsley at the end. There was no time to make anything in the way of a dessert, except if she did something with one of the pineapples. . . .

She was wholly engrossed in the preparations when David Hungerford came into the kitchen.

'Hi!'

'Hello there!' She lifted her head acknowledging his presence. He had changed the Italian suit for a casual shirt and slacks and whatever he had done to the tractor there wasn't a speck of grease on him.

'Need a hand?' He glanced at her, a half smile on his handsome mouth.

'You're offering one?' She lifted her green eyes, at the same time vigorously beating the olive oil and wine vinegar with a fork.

'It might be fun.'

'I can never tell whether you're serious or not.' She turned around, picked up the salt, pepper and the mustard and generously seasoned the mixture.

'Sure you know what you're doing?' he leaned back against the cupboard, observing her with amused, glinting eyes.

'Yes,' she returned firmly. 'What miracle did you work with the tractor?'

'Nothing much. I'm sure it will hold up for the next few days.'

'Hallelujah!'

'I knew you'd be pleased.'

O'Mara, washed up and looking very respectable in a nice clean shirt, walked into the kitchen with scarcely a sound. 'Well now, Katie,' his shrewd eyes flashed from one to the other, 'haven't you offered our guest a drink?'

'I thought you might like to do that,' Catherine returned pleasantly. 'Besides, I want you men out of my kitchen.'

'You hear that?' O'Mara gave a crack of laughter. 'We're being given notice to leave.'

'At least it looks like we've got a good dinner to look forward to.'

'Yes,' O'Mara answered, giving a masterly impression of a fond parent, 'there's nothing my little Katie can't do.'

By the end of the evening Catherine had done nothing to reverse her father's admittedly sardonic remark. To her happy relief everything went off very well. The food was good, washed down with a bottle of wine O'Mara had produced out of nowhere, and as she realised afterwards, David Hungerford handled her father with ease and charm. It was almost like the old days when it had been a pleasure to hear O'Mara talking so fluently and amusingly.

It wasn't until David Hungerford had gone that he seemed to realise they weren't all together again, his family, and he withdrew with a dreadful suddenness, picking up the whisky bottle and closing his door.

Left alone with the dishes, (she had refused point blank to attend to them while their guest was there), Catherine felt a flash of justifiable anger. Surely O'Mara could stop drinking until the harvest was over? But she had seen his blind face, so different from the face of only an hour before. For a brief space of time he had lost himself in the effort to entertain, now his demons were chasing him again.

Bleakly Catherine began rinsing the dishes, then stacked them neatly for the washing up. Perhaps if she settled back into saying a few prayers O'Mara would be up in the morning ready to get the job done.

CHAPTER THREE

WHEN Catherine called in on her father the next morning, it was obvious he wouldn't be doing any work that day. It was useless to try to rouse him, so she had to accept the situation as best she could. Others coped with problems like this and she wasn't going to allow it to defeat her. Neither could she ask for more help—that would be too terrible an embarrassment. O'Mara, though he was a big man physically, was not built to withstand tragedy, and she shrugged abruptly and settled his tousled black head more comfortably on the pillow. She was even thankful in a strange way that her mother wasn't there to witness her husband's sad decline. In many ways life hadn't been kind to her mother, especially when she had been so gentle and beautiful. Just sitting beside her had been a source of profound delight to the young Catherine and even O'Mara hadn't succeeded in weaning his only son from his mother. Patrick had adored his mother, though he seemed to realise instinctively from his early days that he could only show it in occasional flashes.

Once there had been framed photographs scattered all around the house of all of them together, now Catherine alone kept a picture of her mother and brother in her room. Standing beside the window, dressed for work, she picked up the photograph of Patrick and studied it urgently. She was considerably distressed in her mind as she looked down at the young, handsome face. Strangely Patrick resembled neither his father nor his mother. His face was uniquely his own, bright and gay and reckless. Her lips twisted in pain.

She continued to cry, silently, tearlessly, on her way to the canefields, a broad-brimmed straw hat set squarely on her small head casting smoky shadows over her golden-skinned face. It was another scorching day and she had the feeling they were due for a tropical downpour before evening. It wasn't unusual. One got soaked and steamed and dry-cleaned.

When Bert saw she was alone, in his own words, he 'bucked.'

'I tell ya, Miss Cathy, ya dad's not giving ya a fair go.'

Catherine had to swallow it because it was perfectly true. 'We'll manage, Bert.'

'Gawd stone the flaming crows!' Bert bit out irritably. 'I've got the feelin' it's gonna pelt down this mornin'.'

'So have I.' Anxiously Catherine looked up at the brilliant blue sky, feeling a nervous fluttering in her stomach. There were banks of clouds right away over the ranges and they could travel fast. 'Better get cracking, then, and when it's all done I'll see you get a bonus.'

Bert grunted and patted her kindly on the shoulder. 'I'd only buy you a nice present. Ya brother was a likeable lad, but I look on you as someone special.'

They worked untiringly for most of the morning, Bert on the harvester, Catherine on the tractor pulling the huge bin that held the cut stalks. Afterwards it would go to the mill, to be cleaned and shredded and crushed and eventually turned into the raw sugar that was bagged and sent to the refineries.

Just before midday the predicted heavy shower came down, but even then they didn't stop. Bert, cursing and filthy from the charred crop, shouted to her to take cover, but Catherine shook her head. They would soon dry out. She had been perpetually exposed to brilliant sun and heavy showers for most of her life. In another ten minutes the livid clouds would have passed away into the distance and clouds of steam would rise from the cane, from the soil, even from her wet clothes. There was a strange beauty in hard work. Pain. Her back seemed to be breaking. It was nothing. By the end of the day they'd be through. O'Mara wasn't a bad man, far from it. It was just that he was sick.

With both machines working, the air was so noisy neither Bert nor Catherine noticed the big station wagon that ran along the edge of the field and came to a halt at the end of the row they were working. David Hungerford swung out, his dark face so angry by the time he gained both Catherine's and Bert's attention that her heart began to beat at an irregular rate and she could hardly absorb the shock.

'Get the hell out of there!' He put up his hand so commandingly, Catherine swallowed, put her foot on the step and was swung to the ground like a doll between his hands.

'What is it?' she was nearly reeling with fright.

'I won't have this sort of thing, Catherine!'

'If I didn't do it, we'd be wiped out!'

'That's right!' Bert stumbled over, wiping a sooty mark from his face.

'I don't doubt it!' David Hungerford snapped. 'Couldn't you have rung me, Bert?'

'Holy cow, Mr. Hungerford, I look on Miss Cathy here as the boss.'

'That's funny. That's really funny!' David Hungerford gave Bert such a scathing glance he wanted to sink through the ground.

'Gee, I'm sorry. Like the rest of us I 'ate to see her work so 'ard, but she's really got the 'ang of it.'

'Oh sure, you'll be shoving her up into the harvester next.'

'How do you know I haven't had a go at that?' Catherine demanded, without his eyes on her, regaining a little of her spirit.

At this point he turned on her, looking so formidable so devoid of any kindly feelings, Catherine wasn't sorry when Bert moved forward and patted her on the shoulder.

'I'm not sayin' she hasn't volunteered. . . .'

'Oh, for God's sake!' David Hungerford threw up a hand in extreme irritation. 'I take it O'Mara couldn't hold off?'

'Used to be a pillar o' the church,' said Bert.

'Well, it's over for you today.' David Hungerford took hold of Catherine's arm, holding it so tightly she began to wince. 'I suppose you worked through that downpour?' His amber eyes glittered all over her. 'It sure looks like it.'

'Blimey!' said Bert, upset by the whole ordeal. 'I told 'er to take cover, but she doesn't know when to stop.'

It was obvious they were going to have quite a job pacifying one of the most important men in the whole North, and Bert's head fell and his thin shoulders gave a heaving sob. 'Does this mean we're outa business?'

'*No!*' Catherine howled, a fragile dancing figure.

'Stop that!' David Hungerford didn't touch her, but his coldness cut through her rage. 'Take a break, Bert, and I'll send Frank Larkin over to help. If the tractor doesn't jam up again, you should be through by sundown.'

'Gawd, yes!' Bert looked immeasurably relieved. 'Frank's a good man to have on anybody's team.'

'And what am I to do?' Catherine was furious. 'Twiddle my thumbs?'

'Hold your tongue!' From the look on his face, David Hungerford was almost yielding to the impulse to smack her.

'I do believe you'd like to beat me!' Catherine was fascinated by the flash of cruelty, the golden flames in his narrowed eyes.

'I'm sure I can't allow myself the pleasure. Come on, I'll run you back to the house.'

Back at the farm, they found O'Mara still sleeping heavily and David Hungerford didn't try to hide his contempt.

'What a waste!' With one hand he propelled Catherine out of the room and shut the door after them. 'No one can go on like this. Your father needs help, professional help.'

'He's strong, he'll pull through. This is just a bad period.' Catherine was smarting and saddened all at the same time.

'Would you allow me to send Dr McCullogh over?' he asked abruptly, staring down at her small, expressive face.

'And I suppose you'd be moved to pay the bill as well?'

'Don't be bitter, Catherine,' he said quietly. 'I don't know of a better doctor than Andrew McCullogh, and he has enormous understanding.'

'I know.' Catherine turned her face away, remembering all Dr McCullogh had done the dreadful day her mother and Patrick had been killed, and the days after. 'It's just that I don't think O'Mara can stand the sight of him. Memories, you see.'

'Dr Hardy, then. He's a much younger man, but what I've seen of him, I've liked.'

'You can't know O'Mara's attitude to doctors,' Catherine said wearily.

'All of them?'

'Yes.' Catherine didn't wrap it up any better than that.

'Not even when he's a walking disaster?'

'You seemed to enjoy his company last night.'

'That's got nothing to do with it,' he said explosively. 'You must see he can't carry on like this. It's bad for him and far from pleasant for you.'

'Maybe.' She felt empty, drained.

'Open your eyes, Catherine,' he said abruptly, and drew her towards the oval mirror that hung over the sideboard. 'You're almost a prisoner in your own home. Do you *want* to look like this?'

'I can't see anything wrong.' Sardonically she inspected her own reflection.

'In that case why did you go to so much trouble last night?'

'Trouble?' She stared at him in the looking glass, so tall and dark and vaguely menacing. 'You mean I wore a skirt. I didn't think you'd notice.'

'Oh, I did.' His mouth gave an ironic twist. 'If we can ever get you sorted out, you'll be ravishing.'

She still stared into the glass and he frowned and moved away from her. 'I have a meeting to attend.'

'I'm sure it's important.'

'Wait until I turn my back before you stick me

with those little barbs,' he said rather coolly. 'You're not needed this afternoon, so why not go into town? Do a little shopping, browse around.'

She didn't realise he had turned back to look at her, and he caught her grimacing. 'I'll lend you the money you need and you can pay me on Monday when the crop's been weighed in.'

'No, thanks. I'll have to stop myself accepting charity.'

'You'll have to curb that sharp tongue.' They were on the verandah now, confronting one another, and he took out his wallet and withdrew a number of notes.

'I can't take it.'

'I expect it back.' He folded the notes without hurry and put them in the pocket of her shirt. 'I don't want you staying here this afternoon. Is that understood?'

'Far be it from me to disobey instructions,' she returned smartly, and fell back a little, blinking, when he caught the point of her chin.

'One of these days, Catherine. . . .' His eyes glinted with ill-suppressed arrogance.

'You'll dump me in the creek.'

'I expect I might. *After.*'

Excitement flared along her nerves and all at once she was frightened to say another word to provoke him. Her cheeks grew hot and he released her with an open laugh of satisfaction. 'Rather forget the whole thing?'

'Yes, sir!' She whispered it, but only after he walked down the steps and got into his car.

*

It was late afternoon on Monday when Jon arrived back from his trip and rang her.

'Cathy!' His voice sounded young and eager and now she thought about it, lover-like.

'Hi, welcome back!'

'Great to be back!' was the earnest response. 'I've missed you.'

'In less than a week?' Deliberately she held her voice to lightness.

'I wish you'd take me seriously,' he sighed.

'I do.' The tone caught at her soft heart.

'Then you'll come out with me tonight?'

'Perhaps.' It was shameful to keep him in suspense, so she laughed, and after a minute said yes.

'Good. I'll take you to Pasquale's.'

'You've got a nerve,' she laughed.

'Better, I've had a raise.'

'Congratulations.'

They chatted on for a few more minutes, Jon expressing his relief the harvesting was over and done with, then Catherine hung up, her face soft and relaxed.

'Who was that?' O'Mara walked into the room, giving her a sharp, enquiring look.

'Jon.'

'I suppose he wants to take you out?'

'As a matter of fact he does. Do you mind?'

'No.' O'Mara shook his head a little sourly. 'He's not a bad young feller. It's his mother who's the crackpot.'

'Ah well, Jon's her baby!' Catherine gave a wry laugh. 'If she had to pick anyone at all it would be Judy Ogilvie.'

'And how could she compare with you?' O'Mara shrugged, and picked up the evening paper. 'Now we've got some money in the bank, you might get yourself a dress for the shindig on Saturday. With just about everyone in the district there, I want my daughter to do me credit.'

'Will you come?' Catherine looked at her father with her heart in her green eyes.

'Not me,' he said flatly.

'*Please*. You always enjoyed it so!'

'You've said enough.' O'Mara gave a wave of dismissal and went over to his chair. 'The days are gone when I'll celebrate anything.'

'Would you like anything?' Catherine flushed and half turned away.

'No, nothing. Not a thing. Not now.'

All the way to Pasquale's, Jon talked with great animation, his light blue eyes drawn to her so many times Catherine had to tell him to mind the road. As ever, her father was always a heavy weight of anxiety at the back of her mind and his mood had put her out of tune with Jon's careless gaiety.

'I say, what's up?' Abruptly he broke off his chatter.

'Nothing.' She gave him a soft glance. 'Do I look like something's up?'

'You look beautiful,' he said fervently. 'Maybe it's my E.S.P.'

'Point taken, I'll brighten myself up.'

'How's your father?' He gave her a side glance. 'He seemed a little quiet tonight—withdrawn.'

'Eventually he'll come out of it. He's *got* to!'

'He will.' Jon's voice was filled with compassion. 'He just worshipped Paddy, didn't he? Your mother, too, of course,' he added with painful haste.

'No one but a fool would *not* have worshipped my mother!' she cried with sudden anger.

'Oh, come, Cathy, don't be angry with me.' There was a trace of desperation in Jon's voice. 'You know what I mean, and you know your father's special feelings for his son.'

'Yes—I'm sorry.' Quietly she turned her head. 'I know you're my dearest friend in all the world.'

'I fell in love with you when I was only nine,' Jon corrected dryly.

'No.' She shook her head, the weight of her smoky, blue-black hair falling about her face and on to her bare shoulders. 'You love me, Jon, just as I love you. We've been friends for ever.'

'Then I guess I'll have to wait until you can see me as something else.' Jon's whimsical little smile hardened.

Later, as they entered the foyer of Pasquale's, he slipped his arm about her waist and kept it there until they were shown to their cosy alcove, close to the dance floor. Catherine realised this was all going to be very expensive, but obviously Jon had his heart set on wining and dining her.

She lifted her head to glance around, her heart skipping a beat as she encountered David Hungerford's brilliant, sardonic gaze. He had with him the handsome blonde Christine and another couple, a pleasant-looking man and a dark-haired woman about Christine's age, neither of whom were known to her. All of them looked as if they knew nothing about money troubles.

It was a strange sensation she felt—envy, jealousy, neither of them pleasant. Because he was still looking at her she gave an abrupt little inclination of her head, then transferred her attention to Jon.

'This is all heady stuff!' Gently she touched the petals of the crimson roses on the table.

'The haunt of the idle rich!'

'I'm sure most of them are here.'

'Really?' For the first time Jon took his eyes off Catherine and had a good look about him. 'The boss, you mean?'

'Know his friends?' Actually she wasn't in the least curious, mentally comparing her simple summer dress with Christine's knock-out creation.

'Never seen them before in my life,' Jon confirmed happily. 'Probably business associates, but not close enough to get to the house. The fair Christine has a great way of making a person feel little. Do you think he'll ever get around to marrying her? Obviously with her elevated background she'll fit.'

'Who cares?' Since, unexpectedly, she did, Catherine answered a little more sharply than she intended.

'Anyway, not a woman in this room can hold a candle to you!' Jon gave her a cherishing smile.

'Thanks. I was feeling a little ... underdressed?'

'Then it's an infallible way to look beautiful.' Jon rested his eyes on her flawless, summer-gold skin. It was true she was wearing a dress she had made herself with a full skirt and a tiny camisole top, but it suited her perfectly and showed off her delectable little shape. The wine waiter was hovering by his shoulder, so Jon accepted the wine list and if he felt shock and outrage at the prices, he certainly didn't show it. So far as he was concerned he was dining with a princess, and Pasquale's had considerable overtones of luxury and very flattering lighting; the highly personal expression of the Italian credo; good food and superb hospitality. Roberto Pasquale, first and foremost a superb cook, had devoted his life to entertaining on the grand scale and re-educating the fairly ordinary palates of a large community to fabulous food. It hadn't been effortless, however, and only twenty years later was he in the position to build and furnish his dream; a fine restaurant that could be set down in Rome itself and attract the lovers of great food.

Tonight, Roberto was with them and when he found out this was their first visit he insisted they accept the Beaujolais they had chosen with the compliments of the house. Catherine, because she loved the language and had grown up with Italian friends, thanked him prettily in his own language, and even Jon offered a broad *grazie*. In any case Roberto had helped them select the menu which later turned out to be the culinary experience of their young lives.

'Care for a sweet, something light?' Jon looked across at her. 'Venetian strawberries, or Romanoff, or maybe this Monte Bianco?'

'Please, that was heavenly,' Catherine threw up her hands a little helplessly, 'but I couldn't eat another bite! Just coffee.'

'Right!' Jon signalled their waiter. 'I think I'll try a mango mousse. Do you mind?'

'Eat up!' Catherine smiled at his fair, downbent head. 'Though how anyone could put so much away....'

'You've enjoyed yourself, haven't you?' He put his hand out to touch her wrist.

'It's been perfect, thank you. I'd almost forgotten how to relax.'

Later they drifted on to the dance-floor and Jon gathered her into his arms as though he had been longing all his life to reach out to her. 'Did I tell you you're the loveliest thing in the world?'

'Yes, I think you did casually mention it.' She drew back her head to smile at him, surprised by the degree of intensity in his eyes.

'As a matter of fact I meant it, though you constantly pretend you don't know anything at all about my feelings.'

'I'm here with you now. What more do you want?'

'Everything!' said Jon in a faint, husky voice, and gathered her back to him. 'Damn it, Cathy, you're not my sister!'

'A good thing, when your mamma doesn't like me.'

'She does like you.' Jon flushed darkly, but his denial sounded a little feeble. 'But since Father died, I'm all she's got.'

'Which after all hardly explains why she finds me undesirable,' Catherine explained, still deeply hurt by Mrs Morley's changed attitude. She had been very nice to her as a child.

'I think she's concerned about your father.'

'Really?' Catherine jerked back, a sudden passion in her huge emerald eyes.

'Good evening.' A suave voice spoke at the back of them and as Catherine turned she caught David Hungerford's all seeing glance.

''Evening, sir!' Jon spoke brightly. 'Good evening, Miss Kimball.'

Christine inclined her head graciously, but didn't smile.

'Happy about your night out?' David Hungerford asked in a faintly dry voice.

'Perfect!' Though there's no privacy in the whole damned place, Catherine thought wrathfully, burningly aware of her transparent expression. 'How are you, Miss Kimball?'

'You've met one another, surely?' David Hungerford looked from one to the other.

'Hardly.' Christine answered with great coolness, staring at Catherine in a strangely meditative way. 'We simply don't move in the same circles.'

'Then please don't let us force ourselves on you,' Catherine returned crisply, tossing her beautiful head for all the world like a spirited little filly.

'Cathy!' Jon interposed swiftly, and tightened his grip on her arm.

'Well, really!' Christine drawled, but there was an answering flush of anger on her matt cheeks.

'You're really a redhead underneath!' David Hungerford observed dryly, raising his winged eyebrows. 'Perhaps you'll allow me to introduce you now?'

Christine smiled unpleasantly. 'But, darling, I think we've managed that already. I'm very understanding of the Irish temperament, up to a point.'

'They're great fighters at any rate!' Catherine's green eyes flashed, not without humour. She felt enormously excited and daring and expected it was the unaccustomed wine. Christine Kimball was well known to be a haughty, supercilious bitch, and right now she felt as though she deeply hated David Hungerford who was looking at her in his dangerous and ruthless way. Worse, with a glitter of amusement. The wonder was he had ever said good evening at all.

Jon tried hard to put things right by smiling and glancing all round, but inside Catherine knew perfectly well he was mortified and bewildered. 'Please excuse us, won't you?' she heard herself saying sweetly. 'After all, you'll probably want the whole floor.'

She had very little recollection of how they got out of the restaurant and Jon didn't even think to chide her until they were almost home.

'What got into you, Cathy?' His glance had kept wandering sharply from the road to her tilted profile.

'I'm just not capable of suffering in silence,' she replied a little bitterly. 'Why is she allowed to be such an abominably rude woman? It can't always be one-way. She's a hard-eyed, mean person.'

'Nevertheless she's going to marry David Hungerford.'

'That makes me gladder than ever. They deserve one another.'

'For myself, I don't think so,' Jon said seriously. 'He's not in the least like that. I mean, he's a very important man, but there's not a one of us couldn't approach him if we were in trouble. And he's not a snob either, for all his money and power. She's the snob, when who the devil is she anyway? She's rich, of course, but what's that?'

'It accounts for her rotten manner!' Catherine exclaimed, 'Did you hear that bit about the Irish? That was the worst!'

'Well, there's no denying you have a temper,' Jon cut in quietly. 'It might have been as well to ignore her. You know, take it on the chin.'

'So it's my fault?' Catherine demanded, her voice rising. 'I haven't a leg to stand on.'

'Please, darling, don't get excited.' Jon peered at her anxiously. 'I suppose it was the Beaujolais.'

'I didn't have as much as you!' Catherine felt like bursting into tears, her whole evening ruined.

'Here now, you're not crying?' Jon's muscles tensed so abruptly he cornered too sharply and almost mounted the curb.

'Of course I'm not!' Catherine gasped as her shoulder hit the door. 'Don't you think you'd better watch your driving?'

'Why, I'm a good driver!' Jon flushed.

'Of course, you always drive on the footpath. Pull over.'

'Cathy!' Jon laughed incredulously. 'Isn't this taking it a bit far?'

'And don't think I've forgotten what you were saying about my father. You and your sainted mother!'

'Oh, Cathy!' There was a note of horror in Jon's voice. 'I'm surprised at you!'

'You're too respectable, that's your trouble. And don't deny it. I'm the one who's always got into terrible trouble.'

'And it's about time a lot of it got knocked out of you!' Jon fixed her with his mother's resolute eyes.

'Pull over,' she ordered.

'I won't.' Jon seemed jolted by her tone.

'Then I'll just have to knock out the door.'

'This is ridiculous, Cathy!' Despite himself Jon obeyed her from long habit and pulled to the side of the road. 'We'll take a little walk, clear your head.'

'*My* head is no problem!' she said loftily. 'Go home—home. Home to your rightful place with Mother.'

'And in the meantime I let you walk home in the dark!' Jon uttered a vehement protest.

'Yes, Jonnie. After all, we're nearly there.'

'Cathy!' Jon shook his head despairingly, but Catherine was out of the car, standing beside it, looking in.

'Do you mind terribly if I don't say thank you?'

'Darling, I know all about you. You're sweet and you're brave and you're loyal. I love you, Cathy.'

'And I love you too.' The tears stood in her eyes. 'But I'm a mortal enemy to man. They're only out to ruin a girl.'

'Have I ever asked you to go away for a weekend?' Jon cried, affronted. 'I love you and you're going to marry me.'

'No. *No*, Jonnie,' Catherine said quietly. The street had been empty, now headlights picked up her delicate figure in their glare. She expected the car to pass, but as it got closer she recognised its distinctive outline. Of course, the devil himself, David Hungerford. Probably out to rescue the prodigal daughter of a prodigal father.

In another minute he had pulled over behind them and was out of the car walking towards her. 'Catherine?'

There was an unexpected note of concern in his voice, but it didn't make her soften in the least.

'It's his Lordship, then!' she cried, unrepentant.

'Oh please, Cathy!' Jon wailed from the car.

'Is it possible, Catherine, you can't bring yourself to go home?' David Hungerford looked down at her from his great height.

'It seemed a nice time to go for a stroll,' she answered with characteristic spirit.

'Right this minute?' He glanced across the hood at Jon who had swung himself smartly out of the car.

'Why the friendly interest?' It was dangerous enough to provoke him, but she simply didn't care.

'Except that it's late and Jon, very rightly, doesn't want to leave you.'

'To my overwhelming consolation!' She swayed a little and he put his hand on her shoulder.

'I'll walk along with you. No trouble at all.'

'Oh, I wouldn't permit such an imposition.' She shook the mass of her hair back, the light from the street lamp lividly revealing her expression and the sparkle in her green eyes. 'Please don't either of you worry. *Please!*' She waved them both away.

This somewhat amused him, for he gave a low

laugh. 'If you're prepared to leave this with me, Jon, I'll take direct responsibility.'

'What about it, Cathy? Are you coming?' Jon asked with some strain.

'No. No, thank you.' She blew a kiss across her hand. 'I have an idea Mother will be waiting up for you.'

'Goodnight, then.' Jon's tone was offended. 'I'll ring you tomorrow.'

'Not during office hours,' she warned him.

'Goodnight, sir.' Jon addressed David Hungerford. 'You'll see Cathy home?'

'I'm capable of seeing myself home!' Catherine cried mockingly. 'And that's exactly what I intend to do.'

'Really, Catherine, it's quite dark.' David Hungerford took hold of her hand and held it and after a minute Jon got back into his car and started it up.

'What a cruel little cat!' observed David dryly.

'That's not true.'

They stood there watching while Jon drove away down the street.

'And you, why have you mixed yourself up in this?' She lifted her dark head to challenge him.

'Because of you, Catherine. Didn't you know?' His vibrant voice sharpened with sarcasm. 'Come along, little one, don't fight.'

'As if I could afford to when you're breaking my wrist!'

'I'm sorry.' Automatically he loosened his grip and looked down at her, and in that instant she broke loose and ran away.

All kinds of little demons were driving her and she sprinted away until he came behind her and lifted her small and struggling into his arms.

'Give in, Catherine.'

'If you insist!' she hissed softly between her teeth. He was so powerful he could reduce her most frenzied struggled to impotence. 'You must think I'm a fool!' she continued in a rage.

'I don't, honestly!' He glanced down at her face near his shoulder. 'I think you're brilliant—sometimes. Notably not tonight.'

'Look here, I didn't ruin your evening?' He put her down beside his car and she made a play of looking in. 'Where's Miss Kimball?'

'I don't think that concerns you.'

'So I did ruin your evening!' Almost gaily she allowed him to settle her in the passenger seat.

'It's not over yet,' he pointed out gently, and Catherine shivered. That had been said with a most peculiar tone.

By the time he was by her side she wondered why she had surrendered, yet she had almost wanted him to bruise her. Inside the car it was claustrophobic, but the feeling came from within, not without.

'Poor Jon!' she whispered, like some form of protection.

'A poor reward for taking you out to dinner,' he commented.

'I'll make it up to him.'

'Frankly I think you'd better tell him where he stands,' he returned a little curtly.

'He wants to marry me.' A faint smile curved her tender mouth.

'It's obvious he doesn't realise what he'd be letting himself in for.'

'Why, thank you,' she said sweetly. 'Don't feel sorry for Jon.'

'I believe I do.'

Stung, she flashed a glance at him, a regrettable mistake, for everything about him was hard and handsome and dazzling; the strong cheekbones and jawline, the firm, well defined mouth, skin like polished bronze, and glittering golden eyes. The face of a hunter, alert and intensely watchful.

All at once she was filled with a searing despair— an old despair, yet much, much worse than her schoolgirl crush. The thought of David Hungerford had always been at the back of her mind, though these days she never allowed herself to comprehend what it all meant.

'You've missed the turn-off,' she said, and drew her delicate black brows together.

'So now you're going to panic?'

'I don't need to, do I?'

'Not if you do what you're told. Otherwise....'

Catherine said nothing, not even when he pulled off the road and into the moon-dappled blackness of an archway of trees.

'Are we going to have a talk?' she asked.

'Is that what you and Jon do when you're alone together?'

His tone sounded lazy, amused, but her heart began to pound rapidly. 'I'd take violent exception to anything else.'

'And you intend to get married?'

'You spoke of it, I didn't.' She moved her body restlessly.

'I know it was probably my imagination, but I used to think you had a crush on me.'

'You conceited beast!' It was so shockingly true, she literally leapt away from him, to come up hard against the locked door.

'Oh, I'm sorry, then it's true?' he continued in a mocking, reproving tone.

'I think you've gone crazy!' Too late she pretended coolness.

'I remember you when you were just a little kid.'

'I think as it's after midnight, you'd better take me home.'

'Where it's safe.'

'Very.'

'Your mother wanted you to go to university,' he went on.

'I don't want to talk about that,' she said with deep sadness.

'Do you still want to?' he asked quietly.

'If you must know, I feel a thousand years old. Anyway, how is it possible? My father needs me.' She clasped her hands tightly together because they were trembling.

'He might have to pull himself together alone.'

'No, I'll never leave him.'

'You'll get married. Whenever you allow yourself to love someone. You fear it, don't you, Catherine? It alarms you.'

'All right, so it alarms me!' She rubbed her forehead, as she often did when she was agitated. Didn't he know she feared him most of all?

'What, the tenderness, or the brutality?'

Her voice started to tremble despite her control. 'We can't sit here like this. Take me home.'

'So brisk a demand!' Before she could stop him or even begin to struggle he pulled her into his arms, the seat shooting all the way back so she was folded tightly up against him.

'No, I mean it, *no*!' There was a terrible sound of fright in her cry.

'You little fool!' Very gently he brought up his hand and brushed the silky hair from her face. 'I'm only nursing you, like a baby.'

'You don't understand. . . .' she whispered.

'I do,' he answered, and his dark decisive voice sounded curiously tender. 'Sit still for a moment. I've never had such a fragile girl in my arms.'

'What? I can't believe it. Just about every female for miles around worships you.'

'I like deference,' he returned with gentle mockery. 'Only it's your face I'm looking at.'

'I hate this mad moony stuff,' she said violently. 'It's ridiculous.'

'That's because you're a peculiar little girl, and you've had a peculiar sort of life.'

'*Please*, David!' She spoke in a fevered little undertone the tumult inside her threatening her reason. There were tears in her eyes, compounded of panic and excitement, and they glittered in the face she turned up to him.

'What are you expecting, some terrible orgy?' he grinned.

'You'll try to shape me to your will.'

'Yes, break your heart.'

And now she was lost, for he lowered his head, remorselessly, and stopped her mouth with his own.

The reality so exceeded the imagining, it made everything intolerable. She went rigid in his arms, trying desperately to resist, but it was night-time, the wind and the stars and the scent of him, and she wanted what was happening so badly she could have died from the shame of it.

'Catherine.'

The sound of his voice so disturbed her, she was caught defenceless, her lips parted, and this time he searched her mouth so deeply, her own feelings overwhelmed her and broke her to abandonment. She had never expected him to snatch her up this way. She had never expected anything like this—the dark night, the trees arching over them, the relentless passion that left her shaking in his arms, no longer struggling. She had been kissed before, but nothing in her experience had prepared her for the urgency of her own desire.

When his mouth touched the warm hollow at the base of her throat she began to moan helplessly, a poignant, intimate sound that unconsciously invited, perhaps sought, the ultimate sensuality, possession. Though she afterwards flushed with shame at the memory, her yielding body was shouting aloud her desire, her mouth clinging to his, moving ardently as his hand closed over her young breast and tightened possessively.

'Why are you wearing clothes?'

She couldn't answer the half mocking, half serious words he muttered, so shockingly did they inflame her senses. The tips of his fingers still caressed the curve and the cleft of her breasts, exploiting her weakness, and she clutched at his hand at the same time turning her face into his hard chest.

'Don't, please. I can't bear it!'

His mouth twisted. 'You want it and need it, too.'

'Not like this.' Her heart was beating so frantically it seemed to be in her throat, choking her.

'I'd never harm you, Catherine.'

'Then you'd better let me go.' She was desperate now to move away from him, yet her limbs had lost their power.

'Look at me.' He put his hand beneath her chin and tilted her face. 'Have I made you unhappy?'

'Haven't I enough to plague me?'

'*Answer* me.' He spoke so harshly it staggered her.

'Don't think I'll dream of you. Don't worry,' she cried emotionally. 'Tomorrow I'll have forgotten what probably doesn't mean a thing to you.'

'Oh, that sounds good!' He caught the back of her head abruptly and lowered his face to hers, finding her quivering mouth unerringly, kissing her so hard she lay utterly still, half senseless with sensations that wouldn't be put to rest.

'I hate you!' she whispered when he finally lifted his head.

'It's a wonder you don't choke on your lies.'

'I suppose tomorrow you're flying off somewhere to buy an engagement ring!' With a great effort she moved away from him and back to the safety of her own seat.

'For *you*?' He pressed the interior light button and turned to stare at her.

'Heavens, no. How could that be?' She flung him a furious green glance. 'Haven't you already made your choice?'

'Well, I have known her a long time.'

Her face whitened and she seemed all eyes. 'You're a brute, aren't you now?'

'Because I kissed you?'

'You shouldn't have done it,' she muttered.

'Make a game of it, little one. You joined in, remember?' He looked very vital and taunting, the glitter of contempt in his burnished eyes. 'Rest easy, I won't do it again unless you beg me.'

'That's good enough for me!' she said vehemently, stroking her pulsing mouth angrily. Never in her life would she forget what he had made her suffer.

Unbelievably David laughed, reaching out a hand to stroke her cheek while she sat in torment, her head up and slightly averted. 'Is it as bad as all that, Catherine?'

'Please, let's go back.'

'All right,' he murmured with a rough tenderness. 'Now you know how bad men sometimes act!'

She gritted her teeth at the amusement in his voice. Of course he was bad, and deep down inside, dangerous. Not only to her body, but mostly to her soul.

In another minute they were out of the trees and going like the wind. Catherine wondered how she was going to get her shaken, weak body out of his car. It was a cruel blow to know her schoolgirl crush had been obvious to him. Crueller now to consider his conclusions when she had responded to him with an incredible, self-threatening passion. She didn't love him, she was sure she didn't love him. That would be a tragedy. To commit herself, like her mother, to a lifetime of disillusionment. She would never allow herself to be alone with him again.

CHAPTER FOUR

JON called the next morning and Catherine, prepared for it, gave an outstandingly inaccurate version of how she got home. Of course Jon believed her, he always believed her, and finally she agreed to allow him to take her to the Harvest Dinner on Saturday night. There were others who had already asked her in advance, but Jon seemed preferable to any of them. For one thing, she could handle him. She had all the proof she needed of that, and after her experience last night the very last thing she wanted was the ferment of a passionate involvement. She had even pulled the sheet over her head this morning, shrinking from getting up. Her whole mind was confusion and her body haunted by memories that came back to her with shocking clarity. The whole thing depressed her; the wildness that was in her, and it was only a trick, a game. Probably David played it all the time. It took time and experience to develop such a superb sensual technique and that she had come alive to his expectations filled her with bitter acid. She would never play his game again.

'To hell with you, David Hungerford!' she said

sharply to her mirror image, then retreated to the bathroom to run her shower with a loud rush. Now that she had a little money she would deck herself out for Saturday night. She would have to be careful, but she should just have enough. Adversity had taught her the value of money.

In the town, she strolled along the main street looking in the dress shops. There were four, three with reasonably priced clothes and the other that catered exclusively for the wealthy women of the district. Of course there was no way she could shop in there, but there was nothing to stop her from walking in and looking around. Perhaps she might get a few ideas and run something up herself, though for some reason she had her heart set on something rather better than she could make herself. She knew perfectly well Christine Kimball would be wearing Yves St Laurent, no less, and there was no doubt she was a supremely elegant creature, tall enough and slim enough to wear high fashion.

Feeling a little flutter of nervousness, she went in, and immediately a very seductive brunette swept forward to serve her.

'May I help you?' She was much older close up.

'Thank you, I'm just looking.'

'For yourself?' Assessing black eyes reduced Catherine's outfit to one of those cheap little home jobs. It was, as a matter of fact, quite attractive, but the material hadn't cost a great deal.

'Yes,' Catherine said, more amused than annoyed. Unless this woman owned the shop herself she wouldn't be able to afford the prices either.

'Size ten?' The woman studied Catherine's slender, petite figure.

'I'm only looking, you understand.'

'Of course.' The woman smiled in a faintly patronising manner. 'Would it be for the Harvest Dinner on Saturday night?'

'It would.'

'Of course!' The faint smile widened. 'I've sold quite a few originals for that function. May I ask what price range?'

'Fifty dollars,' Catherine said rebelliously, when she knew she couldn't afford it, but the woman looked genuinely shocked.

'My dear, I'm afraid we don't have anything under one hundred dollars at least, and that's cheap!'

'Oh? Then I guess some people are lucky!' Catherine gave a wry smile. 'I'm afraid I just let my feelings get the better of me. Everything looks so beautiful, but I daren't spend any more.'

'I'm sorry!' For the first time the woman looked really human. She went to a rack and pulled out one of the prettiest dresses Catherine had ever seen in her life, 'Especially as we have the very thing to suit you. In a dress like this you could look absolutely beautiful. You have everything going for you, if I might say so.'

'How much *is* that?' Catherine moved forward and touched the skirt reverently.

'Two-fifty, and only because it's a small size. It's from a collection, you know.'

'I couldn't afford it in a lifetime,' Catherine said

regretfully. Serve her right for coming into a place like this!

'Try it, just try it. See what it looks like. I couldn't sell it easily anyway. There aren't too many of my clients with a figure like yours and the sash demands a tiny waist.'

'I'm sorry!' Catherine moved away with decision, her green eyes blazing against the golden tan of her skin. 'I just know what it would look like, but I couldn't possibly afford it ever. I'm sorry for taking up your time.'

'What a pity!' The woman fingered the moss-coloured chiffon with its brilliant mauve satin sash. 'I could reduce it for you.'

'I still couldn't afford it.'

'A pity, when it's made for you.' The woman too, seemed subdued. 'Anyway, I'm sure you'll find something. What about trying Dominica's?'

'I will!' Catherine smiled and lifted her gleaming head. 'Thank you.'

'I'm sure you'll look lovely in anything. Why, I didn't realise when you first came in, but you're a very beautiful girl.'

'It's nice of you to say so. Goodbye!' Catherine lifted her hand and walked out into the sunlight. Really, the whole thing was too absurd. She had simply asked for that, going into such an expensive boutique. She had to ignore her own disappointment. Not so acute when she thought the price of the model gown outrageous. The things she could buy for that!

Head down, rummaging in her bag for her sunglasses, she almost walked into a tall woman who stepped out smartly from a parked car.

'Oh, I'm sorry!' Her voice came muffled and apologetic.

'You really ought to look where you're going!' Christine Kimball said coolly. 'I thought it was you coming out of Cecile's. Amusing yourself, were you?'

'Actually they didn't have anything suitable.'

'I'll bet!' Christine raked her with malicious, pale blue eyes. 'But of course you should have known that.'

'I'm sure I don't care for clothes the way you do!' Catherine removed her sunglasses and slipped them on her nose. 'Good morning, Miss Kimball, I won't keep you.'

'But you sponge on David, don't you think?'

Whirling, Catherine stared at the other girl, outraged. 'I beg your pardon?'

'I gather you're making quite a nuisance of yourself,' Christine said languidly, arching her thin eyebrows. 'Of course we all feel sorry for you. Heaven knows, your father must be a trial.'

'He certainly isn't bothering you!' Catherine returned with grim humour. 'Was there some story you've heard?'

'My dear girl, Dave tells me everything!' Christine looked at her with pitying eyes. 'How you make a little slave of yourself, wearing yourself out. But don't run to *him*, he's unattainable.'

'You're warning me, is that it?' Catherine asked severely.

'I'm sure you have your pride.' Christine lifted her hand to wave to an acquaintance across the road.

'You're making yourself just too ridiculous. Which reminds me, I didn't much like being ticked off by an obnoxious child last night. Dave didn't care for it either.'

'Maybe it's simply that you can dish it out, but you can't take it.'

'You insufferable little bitch!' Christine's pale eyes glinted. 'And don't think I'm not aware of your motives and impulses. I know you've got to marry to get away from your father, but I can't tell you what a mistake you'll make if you ever so much as look sideways at David.'

'You're not sure of him?' Catherine asked sarcastically, inwardly shaking.

'I am.' Christine looked down at her freezingly. 'We just both wish you'd leave him alone.'

'Yes, ma'am, I think I can promise that,' Catherine half turned away. 'I find it hard to believe Mr Hungerford's been complaining.'

'He happens to feel sorry for you.' Christine put a hand to her immaculate hair. She was looking very glamorous in an all-white pants suit and she had added a snappy wide-brimmed straw hat to protect her fine white skin. 'You've persuaded him you're a plucky little thing, but I think myself you've fallen irresistibly in love with him.'

'What rot!' said Catherine with an edge of anger.

'Is it?' Christine returned tartly. 'I saw the way you were looking at him with those big green eyes. I don't suppose you have the sense to realise it's dangerous. David, my dear, is forbidden fruit. Trying to make him notice you is a stupid thing to do.'

'And of course it does clear the field for you.'

'So you don't deny it?' Christine jerked up her head.

'There's nothing to deny.' Catherine shook her head. 'Do you know any more you feel like telling me?'

'I think we've gossiped enough!' Christine said frigidly. 'You'd be much happier if you'd stay with your own kind.'

'Leave it to me,' Catherine returned deliberately. 'And now you really must excuse me.'

By the time she reached the coffee shop she had developed a thumping headache. She collapsed in a chair in the little leafy courtyard to the rear, jerking convulsively as someone spoke her name.

'How are you, Catherine?'

Oh, lord! She could have crumpled to the floor. It was Jon's mother who had put the question, staring at her gravely from the adjoining table.

'I'm sorry, Mrs Morley, I didn't see you there.' And I hadn't, God help me, Catherine thought.

'I should have spoken before you got settled.'

Catherine bent down and collected her parcels and moved to the other table. 'Have you ordered?'

'Yes.' Mrs Morley looked back at her unsmilingly. 'A cup of tea is always refreshing even on the hottest day.'

The waiter approached them smiling broadly at Catherine. 'Hi, Caterina, what can I get you?'

'Just coffee, Renzo.' Catherine met the dancing brown eyes. Being part-time waiter at Angelo's was only one of Renzo's various jobs. He was a highly talented musician and he had formed a group that was just starting to find a lot of work.

'Nothing to go with it?'

'What have you got?'

'For *you*, anything!' he exclaimed, flashing his large, lustrous eyes. 'There's a superb chocolate cheesecake.'

'Perhaps a small slice,' she smiled. 'A handsome race, Italians,' she said, when he had gone.

'Yes,' Mrs Morley answered a trifle grudgingly. 'I'm so glad I saw you today, it's time we had a little chat.'

'Yes, I haven't seen much of you lately.' Catherine forced a smile.

'Did you and Jon enjoy yourselves last evening?'

'It was very grand. Pasquale's.'

'Surely there were plenty of other places. It's so expensive there.'

'But worth it. The food was superb and the surroundings are beautiful,' Catherine said soothingly.

A waitress approached and Mrs Morley turned her head sharply, remaining silent until after the girl had set down her order and turned to go back inside. 'You realise Jon doesn't earn a great deal.'

'He told me he'd had a raise.'

'Certainly,' Mrs Morley fixed her with reproachful eyes, 'but you understand, my dear, money doesn't go very far.'

So now I'm supposed to feel guilty, Catherine thought wearily, and looked up in relief as Renzo approached with her coffee.

'Have you a headache?' he asked her, and gave her his devastating white smile.

'How clever of you to spot it!' Catherine smiled

into his understanding eyes. 'The coffee should help.'

'I have some aspirin in my bag.' Mrs Morley seemed anxious to come to her aid.

'Don't bother,' Catherine said swiftly. 'I'm sure it will pass away.'

'So see you Saturday,' Renzo bowed with a great deal of finesse. 'Good day, Mrs Morley.'

'Thank you, Renzo.' Mrs Morley inclined her head. She had once been very pretty in a dainty blonde way, now she looked faded like a picture hung in the sun. It had as much to do with her ultra-conservative way of dressing as the fact that she scorned make-up. 'The fact is, Catherine, neither you nor my son confide in me.'

'About what?'

'About a great many things,' Mrs Morley said rather sternly. 'I think you owe it to me to tell me what you're planning.'

'But we're not planning anything!' The impulse came to Catherine to leap to her feet, but she could see Mrs Morley was upset. 'What's worrying you, Mrs Morley?'

'Jon is my only child,' the woman said, and compressed her lips. 'You do understand I want him to marry and have a family of his own, but it's important that he should wait and not get carried away with infatuation. After all, he's so young, and he's been my whole life.'

'Are you trying to say he's infatuated with me?' Catherine asked in a quiet, tight voice.

'You know he is!' Mrs Morley looked back at her with very real emotion. 'You're a vivid young creature, even I can see that, but you're not right for my son. Not right at all.'

'Don't you think it's up to Jon to choose his own wife?' Catherine drank her scalding coffee at a rush.

'At the moment he doesn't know what's best for him. He has his whole life before him. I won't allow him to make a mistake.'

'So what have you got against me?' Catherine asked in a low voice. 'You were so nice to me when my mother was alive.'

'Your mother was a lady,' Mrs Morley replied nervously. 'Things were quite different then.'

'You mean we're now the last family you want your son involved with.'

'I don't mean to be unkind, Catherine,' Mrs Morley said bleakly. 'You know yourself, your father is a problem.'

'He's *my* father and I'm afraid I'm not going to apologise for him. Almost any day he can come out of his despair. He suffered a terrible blow.'

'He did. You both did, and I'm deeply sorry, but it doesn't change anything. Jon is so devoted to you he simply doesn't look at other girls. Why, it's almost as if you've ruined him!'

'How cruel!' Catherine bent her head so the older woman wouldn't see the shimmer of tears in her eyes. 'Jon may imagine himself in love with me, Mrs Morley, but I'm absolutely certain I don't feel that way about him.'

'Then tell him. Let him go.'

'We've been friends all our lives. *Good* friends.' Her mind began to stir up painful memories. The three of them—Patrick, Jon and herself.

'I don't mean to hurt you,' Mrs Morley said in an odd voice. 'You're incredibly like your mother, but you don't have her sweet, gentle manner. You and I would always clash.'

'Please, Mrs Morley,' Catherine picked up her fork and put it down again, unable to eat anything, 'I'm not about to do battle for your son. But some day, some girl might. She mightn't be your idea of a perfect wife for Jon, but I don't think that really matters as long as Jon loves her.'

Mrs Morley took a long breath and hurriedly stood up. 'Jon wouldn't do anything to hurt me. We're very close. You're the one who has come between us. It's no good, Catherine, we'll talk later. You've upset me now.'

Not that *I'm* in need of sympathy, Catherine thought, and didn't turn her head as Mrs Morley walked out. Whatever would she do about Saturday night? It might be a good idea to tell Jon and settle it once and for all. A few minutes later she got up, settled the bill at the counter and walked out into the sunshine. She was no longer interested in looking for a dress. Christine and Mrs Morley between them had made her feel restless and depressed— more, betrayed. The years suddenly seemed to stretch a long way ahead. Perhaps everyone was right. She should leave her father and make a life of her own, renounce everything, everyone she loved entirely. Even as she thought it, a single image sprang to mind: David Hungerford. She could see his face vividly and it hurt her deeply that he could be so treacherous.

In a strange apathy she completed her shopping

for the house and walked to the bus stop. It was a beautiful day, but her vision was now turned so inward she was scarcely aware of it. It would hurt Jon, of course, to cancel their date, but Judy Ogilvie was always there waiting. She considered the best way to go about it. Jon's loyalties to his mother were deep and she didn't want to force him to have to choose between them. Besides, it wasn't fair to Jon to monopolise his time. He was her friend, but she could never see him as a lover.

Her shopping bag was heavy, and with some effort she transferred it to the other hand. Who would have thought David would have discussed her with Christine Kimball? Surely there was loyalty among friends? But she knew quite well they had never been friends. Their relationship, at once intimate and slight, had always been charged with other implications.

Distress ripened slowly, now it became an agony of humiliation. He shouldn't talk about her like that. But he had, and the gossip would spread. She had never seen such malicious eyes as Christine's. Head down, wrapped in misery, she went to cross the road. She had already decided to forgo Saturday night. O'Mara mightn't feel the need of her company, but she could always sit out on the verandah and commune with the stars.

Vaguely she heard someone shouting and as she looked up with startled premonition she saw a car hurtling towards her, the driver's face twisted in a grimace of astonished panic. She flung up her arm in instinctive recoil and in the same instant was grabbed from behind and half lifted, half dragged back to safety by powerful arms.

The shock was astounding and she couldn't breathe for the pain across her ribs.

'God, Catherine!' David Hungerford's voice came to her, unbelievably harsh, 'what are you trying to do, kill yourself?'

He still held her painfully tight, hurting her, and she knew a dizzying moment when she had to close her eyes. 'I'm all ... right!'

'He was coming right *at* you!' he snapped furiously.

'Believe me, I'm not suicidal.'

'Damn it, it looked like a classic case to me!'

'Sorry.' She tried to ease the iron grip he had on her.

The driver of the car had pulled up a few yards ahead, now he was running back to them, shouting, 'Is she hurt?'

'No, thank God!' David Hungerford answered curtly, pushing Catherine's head forward. 'Here, don't faint.'

'I've never fainted in my life,' she protested.

'So what's happening now?'

'Nothing. Absolutely nothing.' She *had* to lean against him weakly, his arms around her, perversely taking comfort from the heat and strength of his body.

'What you need is a brandy,' he said firmly.

'Then you'll take care of her?' the man asked gratefully.

'I will.' It was apparent David was angry, but the anger seemed directed at Catherine.

'I hate to think what would have happened if you

hadn't acted so swiftly,' the man told him. 'It was pretty damn quick. And brave. You could have been injured yourself. She never even saw me.'

'While *I* could see it all happening!' David Hungerford replied grimly. 'Why don't you go on now? I imagine you've suffered a shock yourself. Pull in somewhere and have a cup of tea, something to eat. You're new here, aren't you?'

'Just passing through.' The man's eyes were on Catherine's white, shocked face. 'I'm travelling for my firm, Bordell and Co. You might have heard of them?'

'I have.' David Hungerford glanced at him briefly.

'You all right, miss?'

'I'm fine.' Catherine tried to smile reassuringly. 'I'm sorry I had to give you such a fright. I had my mind fixed on something and I simply walked out without looking. Normally there's little traffic on this back street at this time of day.'

'Then aren't you fortunate this gentleman was about?'

'Ah, yes.' For an instant a bitter-sweet little smile crossed Catherine's face. 'He's always around when I need help.'

'Then I'm sure you'll excuse me.' The man's tension seemed to relax. 'All's well that ends well, so they say!'

Before the man had reached his car, without even releasing her, David bent down and picked up Catherine's shopping bag that was sitting neatly in the gutter. 'The car's parked down the alleyway,' he said.

'But I'm going home in the bus.' She tried hard to square her shoulders.

'I suggest you just do as you're told.' He withdrew the keys from his pocket and unlocked the door on her side, leaning in to press the central locking device.

The anger that was in him made him a formidable proposition and she was far from possessing her usual fire. She slumped almost bonelessly into the comfort of the leather seat, staring emptily at nothing. It still seemed unbelievable that she had been almost knocked down, and once more David had emerged the hero, a role that suited him and harassed her further. She should be feeling gratitude, not this quickening antagonism.

'What's upset you?' He flashed a glance at her when they were out into the main road.

'Let's see. I was nearly knocked down.'

'Before that,' he said, and there was no mistaking the command in his voice.

She clasped her hands together and shook her head. 'I'm not telling you anything any more.'

'And what does that mean?' He frowned and his black brows drew together.

'Oh look, there's the woman you're going to marry!' With a great flourish Catherine lifted her hand and waved at Christine Kimball, who was standing on the sidewalk deep in conversation with an old friend. She had recognised the car and looked up expectantly, only to confront Catherine's totally unwelcome appearance and greeting.

The expression on her face and the face of her friend was so ludicrous Catherine felt a little flicker of triumph. 'Aren't you going to stop? Perhaps explain yourself?'

'No.'

'I gather you don't account to any woman for your time?'

'What *is* all this?' His tone was unemotional, but still there was the glitter in his eyes.

'It's just this,' she tried to stop the quiver of outrage, 'do you think it right to discuss me with Miss Kimball?'

'What nonsense are you talking now?' He fixed her with a look that frightened her.

'Oh, forget it!' She could see she was playing directly into Christine's hands.

'I think we might, until you can control those tremors in your body.'

'I'd thank you for saving my life if I could stand it.' She still felt weak and dazed and silky rings of curls were clinging to her cheeks and her forehead.

'It doesn't matter, little one, I assure you. Lie back and relax. You can tilt that seat back further.'

'I seem to remember.' The minute she had said it a flush of colour burnt in her white face. For one blinding minute she thought herself back in his arms, his mouth covering her own, his beautiful long-fingered hand shaping the curve of her cheek, her throat and her shoulder, slipping down to her breast.

For an instant he turned his head and his golden eyes touched her with conscious and dangerous comprehension. 'Last night was enough for both of us.'

'You're so right!' She trembled convulsively and shut her eyes. They were out of the town now, moving towards the highway, and soon she would be home. The events of the day had shaken her so much she settled almost immediately into a drowsy state of shock. She hadn't slept well last night either and when everything fell silent she didn't stir until the car came to a halt.

Then she came alert, staring first at the house, then directly into his eyes. 'Why have you brought me here?' she asked.

'I'm afraid for you, Catherine. You nearly killed yourself today.'

'I know, I apologise. I'm an imbecile.'

'You're pretty distraught about something.'

'So I don't want you to help me.'

He got out of the car without hurry and came around to her side, helping her out. 'I've got to go on to a meeting this afternoon, but I can give you lunch.'

'Look, I don't *want* you feeling sorry for me!' The muscles in her slender shoulder tightened under his hand.

'Me?' He raised his eyebrows. 'Feeling sorry for you? It's a good thing you don't know what I'm thinking.'

'Yes, I do,' she said heatedly. 'I've been told.'

'And I thought you were a bright girl. Come into the house, little one. You could do with something to steady your nerves.'

For a minute she stared up at him gloomily, but he looked so autocratic and capable of bundling her up bodily she knew she didn't stand a chance.

'Magic of magics, she has nothing to say!' He took her hand gently but firmly as one might an errant

child and marched her up the short flight of stairs
that led to the house.

'What's it feel like to live in a place like this?'
Catherine asked.

'I like it.'

'I don't wonder. The Hungerfords have done ex-
cessively well for themselves.'

'Be fair, Catherine, we've worked for it.'

But Catherine didn't answer, walking rather diffi-
dently into the central hallway that ran right back
to the rear terrace. The house was of a considerable
size, planned right down to the last detail, and obviously there had been no budget limitations.

'This must be what's called "living in the grand
manner",' she commented.

'You sound severe,' returned David.

'No, admiring. Everything is absolutely beautiful,
if I might use an overworked word.'

'Come into the living room,' he invited.

'Good heavens, it's huge!' she exclaimed in some
wonder, revelling in the feeling of height and
spaciousness.

'Certainly I could hide you just about anywhere.'

'What about behind that Buddha?' She looked
towards a gleaming seated bronze figure.

'That came from a Javanese temple. Come to
think of it, you'd make a delectable dancing girl.'

'Quite out of character!' she said quickly, furious
with herself for not being able to control her reactions. He had only to look at her, speak to her in
a certain way. . . .

'Sit down, Catherine, while I see about lunch,' he
ordered.

'I don't want you to go to any bother, really.'

'You do.' Very gently he put out his hand to ease her down into one of the many wonderfully comfortable armchairs. 'Afterwards, when you feel better, you can tell me what you were thinking about the minute before you stepped out into the street.'

'Not a thing!'

'I don't believe you!' He flickered another look at her. 'I caught sight of you as I was parking the car. No defences. Just very young and vulnerable. I would have said, badly hurt!'

The truth of it cut her like a knife even if it was said dryly. She leaned her head back and sighed, and when she looked up again, he was gone.

They had lunch on the terrace with Lee, the Chinese manservant, unobtrusively serving them. It was simple, quiche lorraine with a tossed green salad, but so light and delicious Catherine had no trouble disposing of her portion. The crumbly butter-rich pastry was fabulous and though she often made a quiche herself, she had never made one as masterly as that prepared by David Hungerford's Italian chef. Even the salad dressing was flavoured superbly, and the fresh pineapple served afterwards was sprinkled with sugar and kirsch.

'You were hungry,' he said, and smiled at her.

'So I was!' She looked her astonishment. 'I don't know anyone who wouldn't have enjoyed that.'

'I'm glad.'

Something gentle in his words broke down her hostility. She smiled at him almost shyly and her green eyes were soft and expressive. 'Sometimes you're very kind to me,' she admitted.

'So tell me what upset you today?'

'A number of things.' She shook her cloudy head.

'Please don't reduce me to a frenzy. What?'

'Well,' she started off lightly, 'I was fool enough to walk into one of those very expensive shops and take a fancy to a dress that cost a fortune, then when I came out I ran into Christine, who certainly doesn't like me, and for the coup de grâce I had coffee with Jon's mother.'

'And what did she say?' David leaned back in his chair, fixing her with his burnished gaze.

'She obviously thinks I'm a bad influence on Jon.'

'Of course you are, but not in the way that she means.'

'Thanks!' she said wryly, and gave a little movement of despair.

'The boy's obviously in love with you and his mother believes quite rightly that you're not suited.'

'All right, so we're not suited!' she said wrathfully. 'But falling in love wasn't my idea!'

'God, no!' His golden eyes taunted her. 'The point is, the sooner you tell Jon, the sooner he can direct his attention elsewhere.'

'So I lose a friend,' she said moodily.

'Well, you're a difficult girl to be friends with. Possibly when you're both married to somebody else you might be able to pick up the old friendship, but I don't think so. Jon is quite under your spell, but it won't do for a number of reasons.'

'I suppose you think I'm using him, but I'm really very fond of him.'

'Of course you are. As you say, you've been friends since you were children, but it's not a kindness to allow him to think he has a chance.'

'How do you know?' She flickered a look at his arrogant dark face.

'Don't be stupid!' he said, with intolerable prior knowledge. 'I suppose you're going with him to the Harvest Dinner?'

'I'm not going at all.' She looked away over the enchantingly beautiful garden; the swimming pool glittering like a great aquamarine jewel.

'Because you couldn't get that dress?'

'Because I don't know what to do any more.' She leaned her elbows on the top of the glass table and rested her small oval face in her hands. 'O'Mara's not going and Mrs Morley has warned me off her son.'

'Actually, I thought all you young people go in a party?'

'So we do, but we've all got partners. Anyway, I don't really care.'

'Poor Catherine!' He reached out and took her hand and she wondered if she would disintegrate there and then. It was dreadful what he could do to her—fill her with excitement and alarm.

Her turmoil was so complete she didn't see Lee until he was almost standing by his master's chair. David dropped her hand, but her skin was still burning, and as Lee began to speak in a confidential tone, a brilliantly gay voice cried out from behind them:

'Oh, there you are!'

'Christine!' David stood up and turned his head calmly. 'What brings you here?'

'News, darling. Something I forgot to mention.'

The pale blue eyes were darting all over the cosy scene. 'Catherine, how delightful to see you again.'

'Now you're here, would you care for coffee?' David asked smoothly, just chancing to catch Catherine's transparent expression.

'Lovely! You're not going yet, Dave? I thought the meeting was scheduled for two?'

'Two-thirty.' He shot back his cuff and looked at his elegant gold watch.

Lee had already gone off to see to fresh coffee and Christine dropped gracefully into the chair David held for her. 'Tell me, Catherine, did you enjoy your lunch?' she asked.

'Superb.' Catherine gave a calm smile in return. Inside, she knew well enough Christine was blazing.

'Yes, I've sampled Primo's efforts often enough.' Christine reached up her arms and lifted her hat from her smoothly coiled blonde head. 'By the way, I saw the dress you couldn't afford. Poor thing, it would have suited you, but a punishing price.'

'So how much was it?' David asked languidly, and gestured to the returning Lee to pour the coffee.

'Let's talk about something else, shall we?' Catherine said pleasantly. 'It's not at all important.'

'True, but I suppose you want to look nice for the dinner!' Christine's voice softened to sympathy. 'Actually to make amends for the other night, and I hope you'll forgive me, I was wondering if you and your partner would care to sit at our table?'

'What a delightful idea!' David said with feigned lightness. 'When did this come to you, Chris?'

'But surely you'll agree, Catherine?' she touched

his hand and looked to Catherine smilingly. 'David's table is absolutely the best place to be.'

'Naturally,' said Catherine. 'But I'm not at all sure if I'm going.'

'Really?' Christine's expression conveyed her regret. 'Don't tell me it's because of your father?'

'Goodbye, Chris,' David Hungerford said gently, and stood up. 'Catherine,' he moved behind her and held her chair, 'I'll run you back to the farm on my way.'

Catherine nodded, unable to speak. If she did, she would say too much, and she knew Christine was waiting for it.

As it happened, Christine's own smile had disappeared and there was something like confusion in her beautifully made-up face. 'I say, did I say something? I'm terribly sorry. I only meant. . . .'

'We know what you meant, dear,' David said dryly. 'Actually Catherine ought to come along on Saturday night but if she wants to join us I don't know if she's making a wise choice. I've always thought they had a more stimulating time elsewhere.'

'But, darling. . . .' The patches of colour on Christine's high cheekbones testified to her bewilderment.

'Going, Chris?' he returned suavely. 'Don't take off quickly. Take your time.'

Whatever Christine's plan in coming out to the house, it had woefully backfired. She flashed Catherine a glance of such malignancy Catherine actually shivered in the intense, scented heat. She might arouse David Hungerford's pity, but one only had to look at Christine to see her attitude towards any woman she considered competition. Whatever her motive in asking Catherine to join the élite for the Harvest Dinner it could only be to humiliate. Surely she could find something better to do with all her time?

They scarcely spoke all the way back to the farm; neither did they look at each other. Only as she was getting out did David turn to her and say: 'Take care.' In the event the situation resolved itself in some way because Jon, after an awkward scene with his mother, tore over to the farm that very night. O'Mara was on the point of going out and he greeted Jon at the front door.

'I suppose you've come to see Catherine?'

'Yes, sir.' Jon spoke respectfully, biting back a nervous laugh. He had always found Charles O'Mara a difficult, enigmatic man. 'Just making last-minute arrangements about the dinner. You're going yourself?'

'It's kind of you to ask,' O'Mara answered dryly, but said neither yes nor no. 'And how is your dear mother?'

'She's well.' Jon was embarrassed and not a little shaken, looking up in relief as Catherine emerged from the interior of the house and joined them on the verandah. 'Hi!' he said brightly.

'Hello.' Catherine's vivid face softened. 'This is a surprise.'

'Sorry I didn't ring, but I guessed you'd be at home.'

'I was just about to go out,' O'Mara pointed out rather abrasively.

'Oh, don't let me keep you,' Jon stammered, non-plussed.

'I've just remembered my duty to stay home.'

Jon coloured quickly, twisting his mouth down. 'Oh, we won't stay here. I'll run Cathy into town and we'll have a coffee at Angelo's.'

'Then come on, my dear.' O'Mara tapped his daughter's cheek with an impatient finger. 'Are you ready?'

'I suppose so.' Catherine glanced down at her dress. It was baffling the way O'Mara insisted upon the proprieties when most of the time he seemed unaware of her existence. 'I'll just turn out the lights.'

When she came back, her father had already walked down the steps to the car and she knew better than to ask him when he thought he would be returning. Jon called goodnight and she waved, and when they were both in Jon's car, he addressed her gently. 'You know, you're a good girl, Cathy. Your father has grown so hard and remote, yet you're always so sweet to him—the perfect daughter.'

'Oh well,' she ran a hand quickly over her hair, 'I won't say some days it doesn't take an effort.' She swerved quickly off the subject. 'So what's on your mind?'

'Mother told me she saw you in town today.'

'Yes, she did.' A picture of Mrs Morley swam before Catherine's eyes and she very nearly sighed.

'Sometimes I think only sons become an obsession with mothers,' observed Jon.

'And fathers,' Catherine said briefly, desperately

acquainted with the whole subject.

'The thing is, Mother still thinks I'm a little boy. Her little boy!' Jon's face was pale and absorbed with his own thoughts. 'Of course she knows I love you.'

'She's hoping it's just your imagination. And listen, Jon, I must say something. I have a great feeling for you, too, but it's not romantic love.'

'How are you so sure?' Jon asked with a sudden terseness. 'If you let me make love to you, I could prove it. In a way you've always been so sheltered. Even O'Mara enjoys playing the extravagantly heavy father.'

'Well, you see he's not playing,' she said straightly. 'I wouldn't care to be the fool who took advantage of O'Mara's daughter.'

'Please, Cathy,' Jon begged hurriedly, 'you never seem to laugh any more. You used to laugh so much, your eyes shining and the colour burning in your cheeks. I don't like to point out that your father has given you a bad time, but it's true. Mother feels for you too. She believes you should go away for a time, but I couldn't stand that. I can't pretend. You're the most important person in my life.'

For the first time Catherine allowed herself to look at the extent of Jon's involvement. When had his feelings begun to change? It disturbed her greatly that he should have fallen in love with her, for she had found his friendship very sweet and protecting. Suddenly, in effect, everything had changed.

'You're not saying anything,' he exclaimed, without looking at her. 'I know what your grief has done

to you, though you don't even speak to me about—
Patrick.'

'I miss him dreadfully,' Catherine said, something
fluttering around her heart. 'But I miss my mother
more. More than ever, when I'm already supposed
to be a woman. I miss her wisdom and understanding, the way she could unfold my every problem.
Most of all, I miss the sight of her and the sound
of her voice.'

'It's a terrible thing!' said Jon, and fell silent.

Later they sat in the comfortable familiarity of
Angelo's listening to Renzo's artistry with a guitar.
Sometimes he sang his own songs in an incredibly
sexy voice that seemed aimed personally at every
female in the place and other times he just played,
shifting from one song to the next.

'He's good isn't he? I mean, really good!' Catherine put her coffee cup down to applaud softly.

'Yes.' Jon spoke a little antagonistically, since
every time Renzo finished a love song, he stared
across at Catherine and smiled. 'I do wish he'd look
someplace else!'

'It's all part of the act,' Catherine answered
lightly. 'Actually he'd be terrific on T.V.'

'I think David Hungerford has already spoken
to him about that.'

'Has he?' Catherine turned her head in pleased
surprise. 'Good for him! He hands out so many
scholarships for classical studies, why not enter-
tainers with Renzo's unique qualities? He looks
terrific. He sounds terrific, and what's more he has
a *voice*.'

'For my sake, could we forget Renzo?' Jon asked

with faint pique. 'After all, you're my girl, and it's peculiar the way he's always smiling at you.'

Catherine wanted to remind him again that she wasn't 'his girl', then thought better of it. It was no place to do it, with so many people around. A few minutes later Judy Ogilvie and a girl friend walked in, their eyes glancing all around, and as Judy's eyes fell on their table the feelings she thought safely locked away momentarily showed in her face; jealousy, unhappiness, an attraction that had happened way back. For Judy, at the age of sixteen.

Not quite knowing why she did it, except that at the moment she felt sorry for Judy, Catherine lifted her hand and waved. Both girls immediately replied by waving as well, then they were wending their way towards them while Jon turned his head with a kind of helpless anger. Only this evening his mother had been extolling Judy Ogilvie's many virtues, and though he liked her and had in the past shown a friendly interest in her she just didn't rate beside Cathy.

Now that she had arrived at their table, Judy seemed to be in a mild panic, so Catherine got to her feet, and pulled around another chair. 'Nice to see the pair of you, won't you sit down?'

'Thanks!' Susan Hale, Judy's friend, gave them an uncomplicated smile and sat down. 'We just called in to hear Renzo.'

'Hello, Jon,' Judy said breathlessly.

'Hi!' He dragged out a chair and Judy slipped sideways in to it, trying to appear normal but inside pathetically nervous. At the very least Jon could paint a smile over that frown. It seemed easy for

Catherine, who was showing her small, perfect teeth.

'Gosh, isn't he sexy?' Susan's voice carried, but she wasn't the least abashed. She had been concentrating on Renzo for a long time, though so far she hadn't aroused a response.

Judy glanced at her and said in a quiet voice: 'Please don't embarrass us, Sue.'

'Oh, *you*! You'll make a wonderful old maid!' Susan returned carelessly. 'I've got to let him know I'm in the picture.'

'You can do it more subtly than that.' Judy's tone changed to censure. She knew Susan didn't really mean anything, but that crack about an old maid had hurt her, particularly in front of Jon.

'I suppose you're going together to the Harvest Dinner?' She addressed the question to Catherine, with jealousy rising in her throat.

'Of course,' Jon cut in a little violently. Renzo had finished his song and he was directing another little heart-fluttering smile towards Catherine. A moment later he stepped down from his chair and came directly across to their table.

'That was terrific!' Susan offered, with admiration spreading over her whole face.

'Hello there!' Renzo gave a silky, fluid bow. The light was gleaming on his black hair and olive skin and he looked like a Roman statue sprung to virile life. 'You mind if I sit down?'

'Please do.' Again Susan answered for them and stood up to get a chair.

'It's all right!' Renzo picked one up himself and placed it between Jon and Catherine; Catherine to his right, where the light fell in a lovely pool on her face.

Jon, the mildest of young men, seemed as tense as a watch spring, but Renzo ignored him, picking up Catherine's hand and carrying it to his lips. 'All those bravos were for you. Inspiration is a woman.'

Susan suddenly shuddered and held herself tight. 'You'll be playing for us on Saturday night?'

'Thanks to Mr Hungerford.' Renzo shrugged an expressive shoulder. 'Such is his power, all doors seem to be opening for me.'

'I'm glad!' Catherine smiled at him, knowing how hard Renzo's widowed mother had worked to make some kind of a life for herself and her son. Now Renzo would go very much further with David Hungerford acting as the magic genie. Life without music was for Renzo unimaginable, and when she thought how much the Hungerfords had done for the community, it balanced all the cool authority and their splendid estate.

Jon was now looking at his watch and she knew he wanted to jump up and leave. Renzo was a born provocateur, but it wasn't Renzo who bothered her, it was Judy with her honey-coloured hair and serious grey eyes. Catherine dreaded inflicting even a small hurt on anyone and she knew it was hurting Judy just to see her and Jon together. Judy might be jealous, but she had never been known to be spiteful. Once they had even been good friends, but Jon's devotion to Catherine had put a considerable strain on that.

The crowd at the far table put their hands together, clapping and calling for more from Renzo, and he smiled and stood up graciously, very much the prince of song. Jon, apparently, found his attitude comical and Catherine was relieved when Renzo found his way back to the raised platform and started up again.

'We should be going, Cathy,' Jon announced.

'So soon?' Judy's little smile went wan.

'We've been here quite a while,' Jon answered truthfully, but there was considerable irritation in his voice and his manner.

'I guess we'll be at the same table on Saturday night,' Susan looked away from Renzo, delicate as ever.

Judy blushed and looked down at her hands, feeling an almost physical jolt at the thought, while Jon moved towards Catherine almost imperiously. 'Right, Cathy?'

'We'll say goodnight,' Catherine smiled, not very comfortably. Jon was working up to something, not for one moment caring about anyone else—Judy, for example, who wasn't even bothering to cover her deep disappointment.

'Keep a dance for me, old buddy,' Susan called.

'Not unless she traps me,' Jon muttered to Catherine when they were well out of earshot. 'She's a maneater, that one.'

'I hadn't noticed.' Catherine shook herself a little impatiently from Jon's grasp. 'Couldn't you have been a bit nicer to Judy?'

'What the heck for?'

'Common politeness.'

'Have you gone bonkers?' Jon looked at her face in the moonlight.

'Possibly. I don't like to see anyone hurt,' Catherine said severely.

'Do you realise you sound just like my mother?'

They had reached the car and Jon held open the door.

'Really? I'm sorry.' Catherine got in and closed her eyes. There were days, and this was one of them, when it would have been better not to get up.

The car wouldn't fire until the fourth start and Jon wiped a trickle of sweat from his forehead. 'When I've got the time, I'll have to have another crack at this thing.'

'Why not take it to a garage?' Catherine was still thinking of Judy.

'It's a question of money, pet. We spent it all the other night.'

'You insisted after all,' Catherine said in a desperately cool voice.

'I'm sorry, I sure did. Forgive me, Cathy, I didn't mean that. Mother made me mad, and I'm still mad.'

'She only wants the best for you, Jon.' Catherine sank deeper into the seat.

'And I'm quite capable of making up my own mind.' An enormous black dog ran out at the car, menacing, and Jon swore and swerved across the street. 'One really ought to run them down instead of risking getting hurt oneself.'

'I think it's the moment to straighten up,' Cathine pointed out crisply as lights came towards them from the opposite direction.

'Look, don't worry!' Jon's voice betrayed that he was a mass of seething tensions. 'The things you worry about almost never happen.' He steered the car right down the line and tilted his jaw. 'The trouble with driving is you have to concentrate every single minute, and I want to talk to you. Damn! I want to make love to you.'

'It's not on my list!' She looked across at him quickly. 'I'm Cathy, remember, your old playmate. Your friend.'

'And you're blind!' Jon snapped in a curiously hard tone. 'Sometimes I think it's impossible to get through to you. Even our childhood you made that much more memorable for me. You were such a beautiful, gay creature, yet now you seem to fear to express your love.'

'Alas, Jon dear, I *don't* love you,' she said sadly. 'We're only friends.'

Jon never took his eyes away from the road. They were off the highway now, moving out past the fields. 'Face it, Cathy, for just this one time. You need me.'

'I've been very glad of our friendship.'

'Darling!' Jon watched for the turn-off and took it. 'All this being brave, being tough, is just building up defences. Why don't you just let yourself relax? You weren't intended for all work and no play.'

'Speaking of relaxation, it's been a long day,' she sighed.

'You're building a wall round yourself, Cathy!'

'Doesn't everybody when things get complicated?' Catherine asked. 'For instance, Judy is willing to love you, but she can only get so far.'

'Damn Judy!' Jon said explosively. 'She's a nice

girl, and she's right up there in Mother's good books, but I don't want her!'

'I remember a time when you were beating down her door,' Catherine reminded him.

'I was just waiting for you to grow up,' Jon said quietly. 'That, plus the fact that I wanted to make you jealous.'

'Oh, Jon!' She reached out and touched his hand with spontaneous warmth and affection and Jon, over-reacting, pulled right off the road and cut the engine.

'Let me kiss you, Cathy. I'll stop whenever you want.'

'Okay.' She answered briskly, thinking it might solve something for both of them.

'So don't be so businesslike!' He gave a husky little laugh, then wrapped his arms around her, pulling her to him, so her hair spilled over their faces. 'Cathy . . . Cathy!'

There was nothing unpleasant about it, in fact his mouth was very sweet, moving softly on hers until his breathing changed and she pulled away. She was moved, but not to passion, and her body wasn't shaken by tremors. Strange how different kisses could be. Jon had kissed her gently and sweetly, and though she had responded she felt peculiarly removed from the whole scene. Only one man had succeeded in making her burn and ache— a man she hungered for but a man who could only wound her.

'If you could just let me have a little more. I don't need much. *Please*, Cathy!'

She didn't want to hurt him, so she hugged him

hard, turning her face to kiss his cheek. 'You've got to be kidding! I'm a good girl.'

'That's great really, if I only thought we could get married.'

'Do me a favour, Jon,' she said gently, 'forget it for a while. Your mother is ambitious for you. She wants you to succeed before you assume the responsibilities of a married man.'

'I'm all set to go now,' he returned wryly. 'I'd give anything, *anything*, to have you all to myself.'

'So you have. Right now, this minute,' Catherine pointed out lightly, but Jon turned to look at her before he turned on the engine.

'No, darling. Right now, I've got nothing at all, but I won't give up trying.'

CHAPTER FIVE

CATHERINE was working in the vegetable garden her mother had been so proud of when David Hungerford arrived. It was late Friday afternoon and the garden was a living monument to summer with masses of trees and shrubs in full flower and around the enormous gum that partly shaded the vegetable garden, black-eyed Susans had formed a great circle before climbing and garlanding the silvery grey trunk. Nature was lavish in the tropics and the vigorous tomato vines were laden with plump fruit. Catherine grew other vegetables as well; cabbage, lettuce, spinach, radishes and peppers as well as parsley and mint, but the tropical fruits like banana, guava, mango and pawpaw bore abundantly year after year without any attention on her part. It was such fertile land, and working the garden gave her peace as well as contributing to an important part of their diet.

To deter the birds, a scarecrow stood above the rows, and today she had adorned his old hat with a fragrant circlet of frangipani. One for the scarecrow and one for herself. It ringed her dark hair and fell down on to her forehead, but she couldn't see her own charm, only delight in the delicious scent. O'Mara had promised to be home for tea and the thought so pleased her she found herself singing as she worked. The dark red earth had a perfume of its own, the clean smell of freshly ploughed land, and she could hear the drowsy hum of the bees as they got drunk on all the proudly flowering vines. Here, in the garden, for a little while she could be at peace with her memories. Here her mother had worked the soil and here too she had sung. For the first time since that terrible day over a year ago the rawness of her grief gave way to gentleness and warmth. Her mother had believed in a life hereafter, so even now she could be watching over her.

When she heard her name called, she stood very still, the breeze lifting her hair away from her face so the pure, delicate bone structure was brought into high relief. David Hungerford was walking towards her with his lithe unhurried tread, his tall, powerful body surrounded by light. For an instant Catherine saw again her fantasy of some great jungle cat plunging down on her, then he called her name again and it was a human sound, filled with authority and faint amusement.

'Why do you always seem to freeze when you see me?' he demanded.

'You'd only be amused if I told you.' She bent and dusted the soil from her knees.

'Try me.' The golden eyes flicked over her.

'So you can glory in it? No, no, no, no!'

'Then for God's sake step out of that vegetable patch. We've got business to attend to.'

'We have?' He had put out his hand with lofty courtesy and she took it, the touch alone delighting her, though she did an excellent job of concealing it.

'Is your father at home?' he asked.

'He went into town.' The circlet of frangipani was still on her head and she lifted her hand to throw it away.

'Leave it,' he said, as though she were a favourite slave. 'You're the only girl I know who can look beautiful with a dirty face.'

'Perhaps the only ones you really know are puppets,' she answered sweetly, though she would have loved to hit him hard.

'Another dig at Chris?' He glanced down at her glossy black head at his shoulder.

'It's so difficult to pass up.' Secretly she was appalled by the thought of how she must look. The way she always looked to him, she realised—hair loose and wild, dust-streaked shorts and T-shirts, like a uniform. A long way from Christine's pristine sophistication. 'So what do you want to discuss?' she forced herself to ask briskly.

'I'm not sure how you're going to take it.' He gave a mocking little laugh and broke off a spray of bougainvillaea so it wouldn't hit her in the face.

'Then forget it.' She gazed up at him, then stepped up on to a high flat rock the better to be on a level with him. 'What is it anyway?'

'A woman's curiosity. It helps sometimes.' He moved towards her and put a hand each side of her waist. 'Do you feel better up there?'

'Y-yes.' Even to her own ears, her voice sounded panicky. She was so close to him her breath caught, and the hands holding her tightened. If she leant forward she could brush his skin with her mouth, yet nothing about her seemed to be functioning, not her legs or her mind. It was like being held in some terrified enchantment while he was smiling at her, but very alert.

'What are you thinking?' he said.

'I'm thinking I've temporarily lost the use of my legs.'

'So I'll carry you.' Within seconds he had her in his arms, and after the first instant of suffocated surprise she relaxed with mindless pleasure. Everything about him was so unexpected, so enormously exciting, she didn't always have the strength to resist.

They reached his car and he lowered her gently to the ground. 'You must be seven stone at least,' he commented.

'So buy me a good dinner.'

'Do you mean that?' His burnished eyes sparkled.

'No, I don't. You know that very well.'

'So you don't trust yourself to be alone with me.' He moved to the trunk of his car and opened it up. 'Don't you think you owe me something for saving you from getting run over?'

'I suppose I do,' she said a little gruffly, her eyes going involuntarily to the large cardboard box he had in his hand. It was striped in red and white but displayed no label. 'What *is* this?' she said warily, her eyes turning to jade.

'The pay-off!' he said firmly. 'Just for once, you're going to be properly dressed.'

'It's surely not the dress I was telling you about?' she advanced on him fiercely.

'I do hope I've done the right thing!' He spoke with such complete assurance and mockery she could only shake her head.

'I could *kill* you!' she exclaimed.

'Would it help?' he returned airily. 'Ask yourself, Catherine, don't you want to look beautiful?'

'I can't accept it, you know!' She glared at him with anguished eyes.

'The O'Mara pride.'

'Yes, it is,' she returned sharply. 'I can't possibly accept charity.'

'Then I'll have to make it your birthday present.' His mocking tone halted her. 'I want you to wear it, Catherine.'

'Next they'll be saying I'm your mistress.'

'Compose yourself, little one. Who would believe that?'

'Please, David, I *can't* wear it. You must realise that. I know you like playing the fairy godfather, but in the end everyone would know I couldn't possibly afford a dress like that.'

'And *who* is going to tax you with it?'

'Christine Kimball for one. She's already accused me of sponging on you.'

'It must be the demon jealousy,' he answered smoothly, but his face hardened. 'Leave Christine to me and wear what you damn well want. In any case, no one has seen this dress at all except me, and *I* say it will suit you perfectly. Take it, little one, you've dithered long enough.'

'No!' Catherine literally jumped away from him. 'The whole town would be buzzing with talk.'

'Only if you're silly enough to tell them.' He looked at her with a sudden impatience. 'And you're wrong, Catherine, it's not obvious and no one can prove anything. Your father must have given you some money.'

'He did.'

'So give it to me, if you must.'

'How does a hundred dollars strike you? I can get that much together.'

'Just right.' He turned abruptly and picked up the box. 'You've earned it, and it's no gift. Besides, there's always the possibility that you'll please your father. No man is immune to beauty. Be sure of it.'

Catherine took the box into her hands and stood staring down at it. 'This is wrong. I'm absolutely scared to look.'

'It's very plain, really, it's what you're going to do to it.'

'I've no intention of sitting at your table.' She drew a ragged breath.

'That's all right, I don't mind. Besides, all you

young people automatically group together.'

'*No.*' She realised he was softening her up, but her course of action was clear. 'I know you mean this kindly, at least I hope you do,' she said wryly, 'but I'm certain a hundred dollars won't cover it, and I'd be insane to be so extravagant.'

'I suppose there isn't anything else you could give me?' he asked blandly.

'Like what?' Startled, she looked up into his face and clicked her tongue when she saw his golden eyes alight with lively humour. 'You *monster*!'

'Surely you don't see one in every corner? I think you need a little treat for all your devotion and sacrifice. You told me yourself you had money for a new dress. A hundred dollars will leave me very little out of pocket. The fact is, I'm determined you're going to please me for once. After all, I've been following your career for a long time.'

'Very funny!' she muttered, almost to herself. He might be laughing at her schoolgirl fantasy, but she couldn't. For one thing, she had never recovered. 'I suppose you're used to weak women?' she said wearily.

'But you're like a child to me!' Suddenly he dropped his hands to her shoulders. 'I know you're going to grow up eventually and perhaps I'll have to take you seriously, but for now, don't mistrust my motives. I assure you, they're of such purity you'll want to run back inside and get that hundred dollars.'

'What colour?' she asked.

'Now, dear, that's a surprise!' He looked at her

sharply and his mouth twisted in a smile. 'Actually it looks very innocent and harmless. Like you do—sometimes.'

For a moment Catherine stood like a small stricken statue, then with the box in her arms, she rushed back up the stairs and into the house. In doing so, she accidentally knocked a brass ornament off its stand, but she didn't stop. Why did David treat her this way? Why did he try to help her?

In her bedroom she almost ripped the box apart, turning pale under her tan as the tissue paper fell away. It was a one-shouldered silk jersey draped like a Grecian tunic with a side slit in the long skirt. Only the colour was innocent, a shimmering white, for it was designed expressly for draping over a beautiful, slender body. It was young, but it was also very sophisticated and it did the worst possible thing to her—make her imagination take flight. White, against a tan, looked stunning and it turned her eyes to a glittering green.

When she burst out of the house again David was leaning nonchalantly against his car. 'Has something terrible just happened to you—you've gone pale?'

'A hundred dollars,' she said abruptly. 'You'd better check it.'

'I've decided I'll take it in instalments.'

'You'll take it *now*,' she insisted.

'Oh, well!' He put the roll of notes in his pocket. 'Nice to tell me I've got good taste.'

'You've had a lot of practice.'

'On the contrary, I've never brought a dress for a woman in my life.'

'That will all change after you're married,' she said sharply.

'I'm sure of it,' he answered with great conviction, and turned to get in his car. 'Does your father intend to come along?'

'I'm going to try to make him, as a first step.'

'Good for you. Being back among his old friends could help a great deal.'

'I hope so,' she sighed. 'It's been a wretched year.'

'But you've managed.' For a minute he studied her downbent face. 'If I happen to catch sight of you tomorrow, I'll silently toast you.'

'That's all right, I'm not looking for a dance.'

'I bet!' The laughter sparkled in his eyes.

'You need nothing to boost your ego.' She returned his smile and moved back slowly from the car. 'I, in turn, will raise my glass if I see you. And thank you. I *think*.'

Before he could say anything else, she flew off towards the verandah, standing in the golden-green shade long after he had gone until the shimmering late afternoon light deepened slowly to mauve. She was hopelessly, helplessly in love, and she had better get used to it.

When her father saw her in the white dress, such a strange expression came into his face, for one horrible moment Catherine thought he knew where it had come from. But then, she saw it was something different, a look of wonder. And pride.

'Do you like it?' She revolved slowly, trying to keep her tranquil smile.

'For a minute there I relived the past,' her father finally said. 'You know, Kate, one day you're going to be a very beautiful woman. You might give me grandsons. I'll have to live for that.'

It was incredible how he could hurt her, yet she had impressed him profoundly. It was there in his face and the look in his eyes. 'Well, I wanted you to be proud of me.'

'And I am,' he answered, but his smile wouldn't work. 'How much did it cost me?'

'It might hurt,' she said warningly.

'I don't expect a dress like that to be cheap.'

'*A hundred dollars!*' Catherine didn't hesitate, though the colour drained from her face.

'Stop worrying!' O'Mara sighed deeply. 'It's worth every penny of it to see you looking like this, all black hair and green eyes and your mother's glorious skin.'

'Please come with me,' she pleaded.

O'Mara shook his head.

'Please, Father. All your friends will be there.'

'It might be something to arrive with my beautiful daughter on my arm,' he agreed. 'I'll decide tomorrow.'

In the end, though she feared he would every moment, O'Mara didn't let her down. Catherine went off to dress for the annual dinner-dance with so much gratitude and excitement she felt almost incandescent; exhilarated as she hadn't been in a long time. If her father would just stop eating his heart out for Patrick, everything might come right. For a moment she even stood in her bedroom with her eyes closed, saying a prayer. The town was full of good, kind people and she knew they would help her tonight.

Her eyes, when she lifted them to the mirror, seemed to leap out of her face. She had always known they were green, but with a little eyeshadow and her long curling lashes brushed with mascara, they seemed to glitter like jewels. She had washed her curly hair and finger-dried it, and for once it behaved; centre parted and framing her golden, apricot-tinted face in a gleaming cloud of blue-black. She had never really been happy about her hair because it was so thick and curly, not realising most women would have done anything to possess such a magnificent mane. Of course it really needed thinning and shaping, but she couldn't help that. It was the greatest comfort to her, her father had accepted the inordinate cost of her dress, and it *did* look perfect—simple off, but so beautiful on, with her skin shining. She reached up a hand and brushed it down the silky, delicate curve of her shoulder ... dreaming. ... Heaven knows she shouldn't. She was young and inexperienced, yet already she had been shown an almost unbearable rapture. She couldn't lightly forget it, and she didn't want to try. She wanted love and a blazing vitality, but she wanted it from a man who collected beautiful women. There was no sense at all to it, no order or security, only an immense excitement.

When O'Mara came out of his room Catherine looked at him with pleasure. 'Oh, what a fine-looking man you are!' she exclaimed. In his best suit, tall and broad with his black curling hair sprinkled with silver, his blue eyes and his good features, Charles O'Mara *was* a handsome man, and if there was a strange remoteness in those blue eyes tonight, Catherine wasn't going to allow it to upset her.

'As if anyone is going to notice me with you on my arm,' said O'Mara, and somehow produced a smile. 'White suits you.'

'Let me fix your tie.' In a flash Catherine was beside him, plumping up the knot, taking satisfaction in his beautifully laundered and ironed shirt. 'Well now, you know Miss O'Reilly will be waiting for you.'

'I'm sure she will!' her father said dryly. 'Such is her impudence!' Miss O'Reilly, a moneyed spinster of the district, had admired O'Mara for years and never affected to hide it. The family had treated it as a joke, but Catherine had come to see her father was really indifferent to women. The big vein of love in him had been reserved for his son.

Within twenty minutes Jon had arrived with his mother firmly ensconced in the front seat beside him. She didn't come in but remained where she was until they all walked out of the house again and down towards the waiting cars.

'How nice it is to see you, Mrs Morley!' O'Mara assumed a brilliant, totally false smile and leaned in Mrs Morley's window.

'Good evening, Mr O'Mara!' Mrs Morley inclined her neat head. 'I think we ought to be getting along, don't you?'

She intended the remark to be carefully neutral, but it came out with a condescending dourness.

'Yes, certainly, we must all take your advice.'

O'Mara bowed again and stepped away from the small car.

'You'll follow us in?' Catherine laid her hand on her father's arm.

'I suppose I can manage that!' O'Mara answered, and began to walk away to the family Holden Catherine had washed, polished and vacuumed that very afternoon.

'Are you coming, Cathy?' Mrs Morley called.

'There's plenty of time,' Jon said quickly, and opened the back door. 'You look beautiful, Cathy, absolutely beautiful. You take my breath away.'

'Do get in, dear,' Mrs Morley said patiently, 'the earlier we are, the better seated we'll be.'

They were blocking O'Mara's way and Catherine expected him to use the horn, but he never did. As it was, he stayed behind them until they arrived at the splendid new community centre and even parked alongside.

'Take my arm, like a good girl.'

'And I'd be very happy and proud.' The blue eyes that for more than a year now had stared emptily at nothing fixed themselves on her face, their expression vaguely tormented, though it might have been a trick of the lighting.

'I think you mean that,' he smiled.

'I do.' Catherine stood up on her tiptoes and pressed a loving kiss on his cheek. 'I've always loved you, Father.'

'Yes, yes, I see it now.' Gently he tucked his arm around her. 'I don't know just why it's taken me so long.'

The inside of the huge hall was a kaleidoscope of

light and moving colour. The organising committee had been very busy and everything and everyone had been catered for right down to the last detail. This was the biggest and gayest function of the whole year and everyone turned up for it assured of a good time.

Catherine hung on her father's arm, looking around the hall with brilliant, waiting eyes. *He* wasn't there yet, though it was easy to pick out the official table. There were flowers massed everywhere and planters of magnificent glossy leaves brought in from the nurseries and up on the stage, the spectacularly beautiful calatheas grown for their leaf colourings and patterns.

Lucia Zanotta, one of the great matriarchs of the district, with a handsome humorous face and magnificent dark eyes, sailed forward to greet them, speaking with so much panache and immense warmth she succeeded in leading O'Mara away. His old circle of friends was awaiting him and though Charles O'Mara didn't flatter himself they were waiting for him as eagerly as Lucia implied, he knew from their lifted heads and bright, sincere smiles that he was welcome.

'I'm so glad your father came,' Mrs Morley said kindly, leaving her son speechless. 'Your dress is very elegant, Cathy, though I would have preferred you in a full skirt.' She was wearing one herself, hardly flattering to her plump figure, and it swirled out as she turned in delight to greet two of her dearest friends.

'Sylvie! Bette! You both look wonderful!'

Catherine and Jon smiled dutifully, Catherine

sensitive to the barely concealed amazement in the women's eyes, then Jon led her off to a table. 'Don't take any notice of Mother. That dress is sensational! You look like some incredibly sexy little goddess. Where did you get it?'

'Paris.'

'Nice work!' He smiled at her flippancy. 'It sure looks it.'

A group of their friends was signalling enthusiastically, and Jon saw from their faces that Catherine's appearance was dazzling them as well. He hadn't expected such magic himself, so it was doubly intoxicating to know she was *his* partner, his girl, and he would fight off a cavalry charge if he had to. Even more exciting to him was the starry look in Catherine's eyes. He hadn't seen her look so exquisitely alive since the tragedy, and there was no doubt she was thrilled to have her father along.

Some time later, when they were all sitting around the table laughing and drinking a little champagne, Catherine looked up to see David Hungerford arrive. The sight of him so terrified her, she made an unnecessary fuss of inching her evening bag away from the silver wine bucket. When she nerved herself to look up again he was moving slowly towards the main table, stopped here, there and everywhere, by people who wanted to greet him.

To her astonishment he had come alone, probably to avoid the difficult situation of disappointing too many women, and he looked so handsome, so tremendously urbane, she couldn't possibly believe he had even admired her so much as to kiss her. As she had discovered so painfully, it hadn't been in the least lighthearted, and she had trouble thinking of it as pity, so how had she ever for a moment attracted him?

The Mayor was beside him, and they were shaking hands. Everyone around them was smiling in delight and whatever he said, the smiles broke into laughter. His skin was so dark, his golden eyes had an alien brilliance and when he suddenly turned his head and looked in her direction she was so confused, so ashamed of staring, she blushed scarlet.

'Oh, great, it's the boss!' Jon said happily, unaware of Catherine's tumult. 'Now we can get started. I'm starving, aren't you?'

Judy Ogilvie, seated at the opposite side of the table, smiled fondly and said: 'Poor Jon!' Something in Catherine's expression as she had looked across the room at David Hungerford had filled her with a tremendous sense of relief, even daring. Catherine wasn't in the least in love with Jon, to look at another man like that. Not that it could possibly do her a bit of good. David Hungerford was one of the richest men in the whole North and he was years older, able to take his pick of anyone.

The courses, when they came, were delicious and even the speeches towards the end were enjoyable, short and amusing. The moment David started speaking, however, Catherine again fell to shifting her evening bag. It was flashing a million prisms of light and she would rather look there than betray herself through her eyes. She was just too much in love with him, and she was neither worldly enough nor sophisticated enough to hide it.

Afterwards, when the dancing started, she managed to regain her aplomb. Nobody could have been more in demand and Renzo was making it very difficult for her, staring at her with brilliant, ardent eyes, when he wasn't actually carrying her off to the dance floor without asking anyone's permission. Jon was quietly seething, though Judy Ogilvie was doing her best to soothe away the emotional hurt. For a rather shy girl, she was being amazingly forward, so it was hardly surprising that Jon was looking at her with bewildered eyes. He had even stammered when she had asked him to dance.

Once when Catherine saw Christine Kimball in David's arms, she turned her back deliberately. Christine looked stunning. Her dress of black lace had obviously cost a fortune and it clung everywhere it should and was especially good against her white skin. They looked splendid together, so tall and graceful, he in a white dinner jacket with the casual formality of a red carnation in his lapel. It was extraordinary how the rich seemed to have the added bonus of elegance and an understated arrogance. At least, *he* had; Christine Kimball could be very haughty indeed. Some people were better equipped to handle being rich and the power it brought them, Catherine supposed.

Across the room she could see her father talking to a Yugoslavian friend. From his expression he looked to be in a distinctly convivial mood and her heart lifted even as she thought wryly that they were probably talking about fishing. Perhaps more than anything else her father had loved taking Patrick fishing. Patrick had hated these all-night sessions, but somehow he had succeeded in keeping the fact pretty well secret from his father. Ironically, *she* had enjoyed the peaceful joy of fishing her father's favourite spots, but O'Mara considered fishing an activity to be exclusively enjoyed by men.

Dancing with Andrew Walsh left her breathless. He was trying to persuade her she was really fire in her icy white dress and she laughingly pulled away from him, when her wrist was taken by a hand whose touch she would have recognised any time, any place, blindfolded.

'I've looked to toast you several times, but you've been determined to ignore me.'

'Well, it's been some party, you must admit!' Inevitably she went with him, though she could feel every bone in her body dissolving. His magnetism was so powerful, once he touched her everything went beyond control.

Still smiling faintly, he turned her into his arms. 'How extraordinarily seductive you look tonight! Is this little pigtailed Catherine O'Mara who used to be such an excellent student?'

'Don't you like clever women?' she countered.

'Can that possibly mean you?'

'Of course not. I remember you called me a child.'

'That must have been yesterday. It seems ridiculous tonight!'

Momentarily she allowed herself to glance up at him and found his burnished eyes alight. 'I realise you like teasing me.'

'Well now, I'm cured,' he said with smooth

mockery. 'From tonight I swear I'll take you seriously.'

She was clinging to him, she knew she was, fighting the irresistible impulse to put both arms around his neck. Though she had to lean back to look at him, her breasts brushed his chest and she wanted him to pick her up and just walk off with her. It was just so desperate to be in his arms, to have his eyes studying her so she felt warm and shivery at the same time.

'You know you're too tall for me?' It was all too serious, the way she was feeling, so she sought to be ingenuous, a bit offhand.

'Do you want me to put you on a pedestal?' He held her closer, his hand sliding down her back as an exuberant couple almost turned into them.

'No.' It came out like a whisper and her cheeks felt on fire. Surely he could hear her heartbeat striking into him? Too much pressure was building up inside of her, too much wanting and aching.

'Catherine?' he said, to the top of her head.

'Yes?' She lifted her face to him, striving desperately for normalcy, but as she met his gaze she began to tremble and her lips parted. 'Why are you doing this?' she asked sadly.

'Come on, *what*?' The golden glance leapt over her with what seemed to be ruthless demand.

'You know.' The blood was beating frantically in her veins. Maybe she even had a fever.

'It's terrible to hunger for something, isn't it?' David lowered his dark head so only she could hear. The golden light touched his dark face with a pagan sensuality.

'So what is it you want from me?' Was it possible she wasn't the only one to feel this shattering excitement?

'You're beautiful, and tonight you're only made for one thing—to be made love to until morning.'

'And then?' Her green eyes looked mesmerised.

'With you, Catherine, one would have to start again.'

They were still moving as the music stopped, then he held her still. 'Either we leave now, or I'll have to lock you up,' he announced.

Renzo was walking unselfconsciously towards them, a smile on his vivid face. 'Do you mind if I cut in on you, Mr Hungerford?'

'Aren't you doing a bit too much of that?' David Hungerford seemed amused.

'Can you blame me?' Renzo rolled his liquid eyes. 'Catherine is wonderful. Just looking at her gives me the profoundest pleasure.'

'And that's all it can be,' Catherine said in a soft, strange voice. 'I'm going to sit the next one out.'

'But, *piccola*!' Renzo begged.

'Please, I'm a little tired.'

Not tired, she thought as Renzo led her back to their table. *Exhausted.* It would be minutes before she could even catch her breath.

'What's happened to you all of a sudden?' Jon demanded.

'In what way?' She shook her hair back from her face.

'You look . . .' he half closed his eyes consideringly, 'sort of . . . feverish.' There was high colour in her cheeks and her green eyes were brilliant, great emerald pools, dominating her face.

'It's hot in here,' Judy said kindly, somehow easing an awkward minute. 'I'm going to the powder room, Cathy, come with me?' She leaned across the table and touched Catherine's arm.

Galvanised into action, Jon stood up and held Catherine's chair. 'I'll order you a nice cold drink.'

At that moment it seemed to Catherine it was the last thing she wanted, but she followed Judy through the throng, her hand clasped tightly on her sequinned evening bag. Combing her hair and touching up her lipstick might calm her, allay this sense of urgency and apprehension.

'Why bother?' said Judy when they were both facing the mirrored wall in the vast powder room. 'You look perfect.' She said it a little carefully as though she wanted to say something else. 'You and Jon have been going together for a long time, haven't you?'

Catherine turned away from the mirror to look at her. 'We've shared a friendship, Judy. Nothing else.'

'But Jon's in love with you. Surely you've noticed?'

'Would you believe me if I said I hadn't?'

'Yes.' Judy's grey eyes held a sudden warmth. 'You know, of course, I'm carrying a torch for him?'

'Yes, and I'm sorry if you've been hurt.' Catherine looked at the other girl's clear, creamy face and smiled. 'I'm very fond of Jon and I always will be, but it just so happens I think you're right for him.'

'So why doesn't Jon agree with us?' Judy twisted

her honey-coloured head back to the mirror. 'You won't change your mind, will you, Cathy? You'll only have to crick your little finger and he'll come running.'

'Put a spell on him,' Catherine suggested. 'Go ahead.'

They were both laughing as they walked to the door, falling back as someone swirled in, her shining head held high. 'Ah, Catherine,' Christine Kimball said tautly, 'might I have a word with you?'

'Excuse me,' Judy cast a worried look from one to the other.

'You look very sweet, Judith,' Christine said with a curt laugh. 'Run along now.'

Judy shrugged her shoulders. 'Would you like me to stay?' Her grey eyes sought Catherine's.

'I'll be there in a moment,' Catherine said calmly, and Judy opened the door and went away.

'That was very brave.' Christine gave a little laugh, her hard eyes travelling all over Catherine from her head to her toes. 'Please tell me where you got your dress from.'

'You like it?' Catherine asked as though she were interested.

'It's not at all what I expected.' Christine searched the younger girl's eyes. 'Too frightfully sophisticated and expensive, for one thing.'

'I see.' Catherine moved backwards to the door.

'Don't go away.' Christine advanced on her with deadly earnestness. 'I don't like the game you're playing, and I'd very much like to know the point of it.'

'I'm not sure I know what you're talking about!'

Catherine faced her with great beauty of movement.

'Oh yes, you do!' Christine gave her no chance to get away, holding her hand on the door. 'You're just flinging yourself at Dave, and I don't like it.'

'What an arrogant person you are!' Catherine said sharply. 'Sneering at everyone in your superior way. I am not *flinging myself* at David Hungerford, as you call it, and I can't see how it's any of your business even if I were. You may have everything else you want, but you don't have him!'

'Oh yes, I do!' Christine flung up her head in a proud, angry fashion. 'Why do you suppose I'm so frantic trying to settle you and him? What Dave feels for me is a genuine passion and I won't be humiliated by a little upstart like you. Dave and I have been lovers for a long time. His nature might require more than one woman, but he's going to marry me!'

'Then I wish you great happiness!' Catherine burst out in violent revulsion.

'Forget your damned happiness—keep away from Dave!' Tears came into Christine's eyes, tears of rage, and she didn't even seem to care she was shouting.

Someone pushed against the door, and Christine had to stand back to let them in, positioning herself at the mirror as though fixing her hair.

'End of lecture,' Catherine said quietly, and slipped out the door as two young girls, slim as tulips, came in in a laughing flurry.

It was impossible to enjoy herself after that. So he used people to fill in a bored moment? Did it have to be *her*? She couldn't feel the pain yet for the deadening sensation around her heart; she heard Christine's voice again, ragged with emotion: *Dave and I have been lovers* ... and wouldn't he do it beautifully, a past master of the art of seduction? No wonder Christine was sick with jealousy; she was entitled to be—possessed for so long by a man who would marry her in his own good time.

'What's wrong, Cathy?'

She was dancing with Jon and he was brushing his mouth against her cheek.

'Nothing.' She turned her face and tried to smile at him.

'You look so remote.'

'As a matter of fact I'm finding it a bit boring,' she confessed.

'Oh, really?' He looked hurt. 'You don't look bored, exactly. More like you're thinking murky thoughts.'

'Maybe I am.' Without wishing it, she had just caught sight of David and he had raised his glass to her, his amber eyes half closed. You *rotter!* she thought, all in a rush. You *black-hearted rotter!* Not that he had kissed her forcibly, or drugged her. Her own feelings had overwhelmed her.

'Cathy?' Jon said again, looking anxiously into her perfect, withdrawn face. 'If you're that fed-up, we'd better go home.'

'No, you stay,' she said, a little curtly. 'I don't intend to ruin your night.'

'You've done that already,' Jon said pointedly. 'Gosh, you're a girl of extremes. When we arrived, you seemed on top of the world, now you're ecstatic to get away.'

'O'Mara's tired,' she said, catching a glimmer of her father's face. 'He'll be glad to go home.'

'Oh God, I can't stop you. You're a free agent, but must you make me so unhappy?' Jon held her so tightly she winced in pain. 'Please, Cathy. I don't care if we go, but please let's go together. I'll probably finish up taking a swipe at Renzo anyway. He's been driving me mad all night, though I know you've been doing nothing to entice him.'

Catherine was hardly listening to a word he was saying. David was standing up, holding Christine's chair, and it aroused a kind of desperation in her. A little hell she had made for herself. He would disclaim all responsibility. Fearing her expression would give her away, she pulled out of Jon's arms and walked off the floor.

'Darling!' he caught her elbow, utterly bewildered.

'I'm sorry, Jon.' She couldn't face another minute in the same hall. 'If my father wants to go home, I'm going.'

'But he's having a good time!' Jon searched the crowd for Charles O'Mara's distinctive head. He looked flushed, and a little agitated, and Catherine rushed across the room to her father's side.

Her first reaction was that her father had drunk too much, then she saw he looked perfectly sober but ill, his eyes glazed, the expression turned inwards as though he were listening to his own body.

'Are you all right, Father? Would you like to go home now?' Catherine laid her hand on his arm, a weight of anxieties pressing in on her. For most of the evening as she checked on her father, he had looked happy and relaxed, now she was at a loss to understand the quick change in him, as sudden as her own.

'I think I might!' Unexpectedly O'Mara leant on her, his big voice barely above a whisper. 'I've got this damnedest feeling.'

'Are you all right there, Charlie?' Jock McClary, an old friend standing talking a few feet away, turned back to them.

'A little strange.' O'Mara stood perfectly still, as though he couldn't trust himself to walk.

'Och, man, what's the matter with you?' Jock experiencing shock, surged forward quickly, and as he started towards them, obviously alarmed, other people turned around from their tables and seeing O'Mara standing so rigidly got up in a hurry.

'*Father*?' Catherine's heart had begun to hammer and as she stood there in helpless horror, her father, breathing harshly, clutched at his chest and pitched forward so heavily she couldn't hold him, nor could the small, wiry Jock break his fall.

Someone screamed. Not Catherine, who was beside her father on the floor. He looked ghastly, and as she went to move his head she was lifted away bodily as David Hungerford cleared the area and Doctor McCullogh dropped to his knees beside the stricken man.

'Heart attack,' he said briefly, clearing the victim's airways and preparing to give mouth-to-mouth resuscitation. 'Get an ambulance here, Dave, on the double!'

CHAPTER SIX

CATHERINE went in the ambulance, trembling so violently she was given a sedative as soon as they arrived at the hospital. There her father was wheeled away from her, his pallor so shocking she wondered if she was ever going to see him again. He had been conscious in the ambulance and she had held his hand, seeing the expression of relief in his eyes. The hospital had an excellent cardiac unit and Doctor McCullogh was a very good doctor.

A nurse led her away to the waiting room, but before she had sat down, David arrived.

'Catherine, are you all right?'

'Yes,' she said bleakly, and sank into a chair.

'I'll bring some tea,' the nurse offered, colouring as David Hungerford looked at her.

'Fine.' He glanced back at her absently and she went off to attend to it.

'What's happening?' Catherine asked unhappily. Her teeth were chattering so much, he whipped off his jacket and put it around her shoulders.

'Your father's in good hands.' He sat down beside her. 'Doctor McCullogh should be back in a little while. We'll know more then.'

'Thank you for coming.' She shook her head in pain.

'They've given you something?' he asked, his brilliant gaze intent.

She nodded. 'I couldn't seem to stop trembling.'

'You're still doing it.' He put his hand over hers as though willing her some of his hard strength. 'One way and another, you've had hell.'

She heard his words in a daze of shock, but his hand on hers had a steadying effect. She heard footsteps behind them and the nurse was back, setting her tray down on the table. 'I've brought one for you, Mr Hungerford.' She was young and pretty and her quick looks and high colour betrayed her.

'Thank you,' his voice was low, 'I'll attend to it.'

'I don't want any.' Catherine stared at the floor. 'I don't think I can swallow.'

'Try for me.' He stood up and put his hand lightly on her head. 'Your father's going to be all right.'

'Then why don't they let me see him?'

'He's probably been sedated. Try not to worry Catherine. I know it's hard, but people come back from heart attacks every day. Your father is a strong man.'

'He's fifty-two, and this last year hasn't helped him one bit——'

'Drink this,' he said, and stood by her.

It seemed easier to obey, and strangely enough the simple act of drinking brought a degree of calmness to her thoughts. 'Of all the nights for it to happen!'

'Doctor McCullogh was immediately on hand. It may have been a mild attack.'

'I don't think so.' Her hand began to tremble violently and he took the empty cup from her. 'You don't have to wait with me.'

'I could beat you for that,' he said softly, and

reached out and took her hand again.

When Doctor McCullogh came back they both jumped to their feet, Catherine taking a stumbling step forward. 'How is he, Doctor?'

For a moment the doctor didn't answer, his clever, kindly face as blanched as his white coat. 'We did everything we could, Cathy.'

She should have known it from the pity in his eyes, the way he tried to frame the sentence, one hand half lifted and extended towards her.

'I'm so deeply sorry, my dear. Your father just slipped away from us without a fight.'

'No!' She shouted it at him, her green eyes staring, swallowing up her face. 'It isn't true! It can't be true—not after Mother and Patrick. He couldn't die just like that!'

'I'm sorry ... sorry.' The doctor was moving towards her. Strong arms were cradling her, yet she felt dizzy and cold. Her head began to turn from side to side, her body trembling convulsively as she went into severe shock. So many frightening sensations, and too much for her strength. She could feel herself slipping into a blurred fog, no longer responding to the voices around her, then mercifully blackness claimed her and the blackness remained.

When she awoke, she was in a room by herself and sunlight was pouring through the window. Now her memory surged back and she was crying in earnest.

'My dear.'

She turned her head on the pillow and a nursing Sister was there, an older woman with wonderful blue eyes.

She couldn't answer and the Sister seemed to realise this, for she put out her hand and stroked Catherine's hair away from her brow. 'There's a saying that none of us is given more than we can bear. You must be a strong, brave girl, Catherine?'

'No.' Catherine shook her head brokenly.

'Do you want to talk about it?' The woman pulled up a chair to the bed. 'I want to help you, Catherine, if you'll let me. I have daughters of my own and they too lost their father.'

'I'm sorry.' Catherine made a helpless little gesture with her hand that upset the other woman for all her training. In the morning light Catherine's young face was ravaged, the lips twisted in pain. She began to talk, the words pouring out disjointedly, and Sister Raymond listened and occasionally added words of her own. After about ten minutes Catherine stopped talking abruptly.

'You've been very kind to me, Sister, sharing my burden.'

'It's easier when we know we're not alone.' Sister Raymond stood up, her blue eyes compassionate. There was a little colour in the girl's cheeks and she said soothingly, 'I'll come back.'

Before Catherine was ready to go home, Doctor McCullogh spoke to her in his office, as friend and doctor, watching her keenly and keeping her talking until David arrived.

Catherine had obviously not expected him, for she swayed a little and seemed to forget Doctor McCullogh's presence.

'There's no need to worry about me. No need at all.'

He only looked at her directly and his gaze didn't waver. 'What little I can do, I intend to.'

She gave a strange little laugh, dressed in her shining white dress again because that was all she had. 'You see, Doctor, David Hungerford gets everything he wants.'

'He does care, Cathy, and that's what really matters.' Doctor McCullogh walked with them to the main door of the hospital. 'I'm worried about you staying alone at the farm.'

'She's not.' David turned his dark head. 'That's the end of the farm so far as Catherine is concerned.'

'Goodbye, Doctor,' Catherine said gently. 'You see how he seems to like rearranging my life.'

'*Dave*?' the doctor's eyes turned to the man he respected and whom he called on endlessly for help.

'I'll be in touch!' David looked back at the doctor straightly. 'Very probably today.'

'Right.' The doctor lifted his hand in salute, apparently satisfied. 'I'm here, Cathy, whenever you need me. You know that, don't you?'

'Yes, Doctor, thank you.' Catherine heard her own voice speaking, but it sounded faraway and aloof.

The Jaguar was parked where it shouldn't have been; right outside the door, but Catherine didn't see anything remarkable in that. A lot of Hungerford money had gone into the building of the hospital and the new private wing.

She let David put her in the car, her green eyes burning in her colourless face, her back straight and slender in the seat instead of relaxing. Like Doctor McCullogh she knew he was looking at her keenly, but she never turned her head. She was finished, spent, with no little schoolgirl's heart to go pit-a-pat.

'Where are you dragging me off to?' she asked him without turning her head.

'Home.'

'How foolish, though I don't care.'

'My aunt Edith flew in this morning. She'll be staying at the house.'

'I understand—a chaperone.' With him it seemed easier to talk derisively than bear the pain. 'So you do have a few twinges of conscience.'

'Deflect your pain at me, little one,' he drawled. 'I can take it.'

'I suppose you won't let me go back to the farm?'

'Do you want to?' He looked at her frozen little profile.

'No.' She glanced down at her knotted hands. They were clasped together so tightly the knuckles were white. 'I've lost everything in this world I loved.'

'Yes,' he said abruptly. 'There've been too many tragedies in your life.'

'There was nearly another,' she told him. 'I thought I was in love with you.'

'And now you're not.'

'No.' She felt cruel and cold. 'You might just as well be dead to me.'

'Then why not stay at my home as anywhere else? I've got business to attend to, a few inter-state trips. You'll see very little of me.'

'And a great deal of your aunt.'

'You may come to like her.'

'Not if she's like you.' In her grief she was fixing

all her helpless rage on him.

'She's not in the least like me,' he said firmly. 'She's quiet and calm and gentle. You don't have to be together all the time. You're free to do whatever you want.'

Catherine laughed incredulously with more than a touch of hysteria. 'And it's all because you're sorry for me, is that it?'

He shook his head, parked off the road and turned to her slowly. 'When you're ready, I'm going to marry you.'

'You're *what*?' She shrank away from him and a low whisper rose in her throat.

'You said yourself I get everything I want,' he reminded her with harsh gravity.

'Not *me*.' Her voice sounded broken, and though she strained away, he pulled her into his arms.

'I've wanted you for a long time and I've promised myself I'd wait. Now we don't have the time.' He was staring at her sombrely and he looked very grim and formidable.

'Don't you think I deserve someone who cares for me?' she cried, her eyes darkened with intensity to jade.

'I can't even suggest caring, can I?' He met her beautiful, pained eyes. 'I *am* certain I can look after you, so I'm going to marry you very soon.'

'You're insane!' She was too weak to struggle, even to speak.

'Perhaps I am.' He lifted his hand and brushed her cheek. 'You can hurt me, Catherine, and you're finding it out all at once.'

'And if I won't?' She stared at him, overcome by

a sense of complete unreality.

'You will,' he said, and his voice was quiet and indomitable. 'It's not possible for you to get away from me and you're so exhausted you won't even try.'

It rained the day of the funeral and Catherine stood at the graveside, her hands clenched tightly together, her young face stark and drawn. There were no tears left in her. She had cried right through the night with a painful passion and her eyelids were still red and heavy. David stood near her, his aunt on the other side, and ringed right around them were the kindhearted people of the town. Charles O'Mara's sudden death had shocked them all and they were all deeply sorry for his child. Catherine wasn't aware of it, but she was, in fact, very much liked and most people had already decided they would help her in any way they could. Of course it would be impossible for her to keep on the farm, but they all seemed to remember she had done very well at school. Perhaps a fund could be organised to send her to university.

Catherine stood there uncaring of any of their plans. In her stunned state, it was even acceptable that her life had been decided for her. She had been devastated too much in her life, now she never wanted to love again. Romance was for the very young, but she was terribly terribly old.

Afterwards she was tired and said she wanted to be alone. Jon had tried to speak to her, and at his dear, familiar face, she could hardly stop herself from bursting into tears. She knew he had wanted to go with her to the hospital and she remembered how she had told him he would only be in the way. She couldn't bear to see him so upset and she knew now that she had always been the strong one in their relationship. A woman needed a man to lean on and she knew, for all her desolation, that David Hungerford was cold steel.

A week slipped by, then two, all the while isolated at the house. Edith Hungerford was a very kind, considerate woman, so obviously devoted to her nephew that Catherine was certain she would have done anything he asked. As it was, she made no demands upon Catherine, always there when she wanted her, a sympathy and concern in her fine dark eyes that took no words to convey. So life went by quietly, the household running smoothly, and none of it making sense to Catherine. Let David make his plans for the future. She couldn't stop him because she was incapable of action.

One late afternoon when she was returning from a walk, she saw Jon's car parked on the edge of the Hungerford estate. He must have been waiting for her, because he jumped out of the small vehicle and raced towards her with a look of deep anxiety.

'Cathy!'

She turned her darkened eyes to him. 'Jon, what are you doing here?'

'It's as close to you as I can get.' He took her by the arms and stared into her face. 'You've lost weight. There's nothing of you.'

'I'm alive. I eat and sleep.'

'I've been frantic with worry.' He put up his hand and rested it on her cheek. 'How are you?'

'I'm unable to say exactly.'

'You mustn't lose heart, Cathy.' He had a deep frown on his face.

'I haven't got one.' She looked away vaguely.

'What's happening about the farm?' Jon asked. 'I mean, when are you coming home?'

'You'll have to ask David.'

'*David?*' said Jon in a terrible voice. 'He can't shelter you for ever.'

'Really, he seems to think so.' Catherine turned on him and she sounded a little hysterical. 'He wants to marry me.'

Jon was so stunned he didn't know how to answer. Then finally he gripped her hard. 'He *can't*! You love me.'

'I don't love anyone, I just want to be alone.'

'It's the shock.' Jon was still holding her firmly, distressed at the fragility of her bones. 'You need time to recover.'

'When do I get to do that? Maybe never.'

'You will, Cathy, because you're young. Please let me see you, talk to you.'

'Of course. I'll ring you.' She spoke to him gently, but her green eyes were already looking away from him.

'I'm worried about you. Lots of people are worried about you.'

'Why?' She looked at him in astonishment. 'I'm being killed with kindness.'

Jon's expression turned to despair and he looked away to where a car was gaining on them rapidly. 'It's Hungerford.'

'It's his road.'

'You can't really mean what you said, Cathy.' All at once Jon's voice grew angry. 'He can't possibly want to marry you. To my knowledge he's got enough of a problem with Christine Kimball.'

'He wants *me*. For his own reasons.'

'God!' Jon looked into her eyes for a long moment. 'Is it possible you're being brainwashed?'

'Ask him.' Catherine looked towards the car, watching David swing out.

'Hello, Catherine. Jon.' His voice was quite calm, but his eyes were very alive.

'Good afternoon, Mr Hungerford.' Jon alone responded. 'I just wanted to have a word with Cathy.'

'Why not come up to the house?'

'I had something different in mind,' Jon said bravely.

'Well, Catherine's free to do whatever she likes.'

'Is she?' Jon burst out in a jealous rush, when normally he wouldn't have dared. 'She seems more like a prisoner to me.'

'I'll forget that, Jon,' David said mildly, though his expression said he thought the young man a perfect fool. 'Nothing very much is touching Catherine at the moment.'

'Then you'll allow her to speak for herself?' Something was driving Jon relentlessly and he turned violently to stare into Catherine's curiously rapt face. She was following the flight of a bird, withdrawn from a discussion that did not matter. The sun struck blue lights into her cloud of black hair, and her eyes were raised and glowing like emeralds. 'Cathy?' He was baffled and distressed at the change in her. She had endured to much, now she truly did have the air of a prisoner, robbed of all spirit. 'Would you like to come with me now? I'll take you home to Mother.'

The faintest smile curved her mouth and she touched his sleeve briefly. 'Dear Jon,' she said with gratitude.

'Then you'll come?'

'I'm sorry, Jon,' said David as though he didn't know why the younger man had asked the question. 'Perhaps another time.'

'I don't understand.' Jon made an aimless little gesture with his hand. 'Catherine tells me you intend to marry her?'

'I do.' There was something inexorable about the answer and still Catherine stood quietly.

'It's impossible.'

'Why?' David waited, a man with whom everyone was very respectful.

'You must know she doesn't love you?'

'Yet she's marrying me of her own wish.' The golden eyes glinted, the tall body surrounded by an actual aura of power.

'Cathy?' Jon exclaimed, and looked back at Catherine incredulously.

She shook her head slowly. 'I'm tired, David.'

'Then I'll take you back up to the house.' He moved towards her and drew her under his arm. No escape.

'Listen to me, Cathy,' Jon pleaded. 'You must listen!'

'I'm sorry, Jon.' David gave him a brief look. 'I understand too well how you're feeling, but you'll have to learn how to let go. You're no longer children and you convinced yourself Catherine shared your feelings. She doesn't.'

'She's ill.'

'No, she isn't. She's still in shock.'

Jon was about to embark upon another remark, but David turned away from him as though he had had more than enough. So Jon shook his head and with a firmly compressed mouth marched back to his car. If Catherine married David Hungerford, she would regret it for the rest of her days.

But the community, when they heard about it, accepted the news with the greatest delight. They thought it hugely romantic. Catherine O'Mara was a very beautiful girl and it was about time she was treated to the good life. A few resented the news bitterly, but as David Hungerford was such a power in the North, they didn't openly express their views. His name had been coupled with many attractive women, notably of late Christine Kimball, but she apparently didn't care, for she had got herself engaged to an enormously rich man almost old enough to be her father.

Catherine was deeply uncaring. One evening after dinner, when they were sitting out on the terrace, David pitched away his cigarette and turned to her with a firm air of purpose. She looked undeniably beautiful in a misty green dress, but he had been quick to note she had scarcely eaten a thing at dinner.

'Catherine?'

She heard his voice, quiet but implacable.

'Yes?' She tilted her head back to answer him.

'I'm sending you away for a month or two.'

'Oh.' She didn't ask where.

'I've let you drift quietly because you needed to, now I think you need a change.'

'On my own?'

'No.' He reached out a hand and caught hold of her wrist, imprisoning it so that she had to look up at him. 'You get on well with Edith and she's fond of you, I know. I think you need a holiday, a change of scene.'

'Don't worry,' she said briefly, not wanting the warm pressure on her wrist.

'But I do.' He was studying her with the analytical detachment of a stranger. 'Edith will take you back with her to Sydney. She has a beautiful home on the harbour and a wide circle of friends. She can take you places you've never been, introduce you to my young cousins—there are four of them about your age. If you'll allow yourself, you'll enjoy it.'

'No, I can't go,' she said shakily.

'Surely not because you can't bear to leave me?' His eyes struck down rather grimly on her exquisite young face.

'It's pleasant here,' she managed, low-voiced.

'You think about your pain all the time.'

'So?' She got up from her chair sharply, making an evasive gesture as he got up too, towering over her.

'So I'm not going to let it continue.'

The memory of what once had been between them made her momentarily close her eyes. For weeks now, this was the nearest she had come to life, and quite unexpectedly she burst into tears and ran

away across the garden. It was painful to feel anything, too painful—and there had been something
in his eyes. For weeks her grief had been her ob-
livion, but it wasn't strong enough to blot out her
memories.

The summer house was a refuge, but before she
could reach it, David had caught her up easily,
swinging her up bodily into his arms.

She shuddered and fought him, finding herself in
great danger, but he didn't even hesitate, moving
into the detached garden room and lowering her
down with him into the deep, soft, comfortable sofa
that almost ringed the vine-wreathed circular structure.

'Stop it,' he said harshly, and took her head tightly
between his hands.

'You can't. I won't let you!' Moonlight was pouring through the latticework and she could see the
disturbed glitter of his eyes.

'I need to,' he answered tautly. 'Even you should
be able to see that.'

'I'll scream,' she whispered frantically. 'You've
never touched me, ever. Not all these long weeks.'

'But I want to touch you now.'

It was like dragging herself out of a dream; ter-
rifying and at the same time so violently thrilling,
she just couldn't bear it. She was beset by fright, the
primitive reaction of the female against the all-
conquering male.

When he lowered his head she closed her eyes,
arching her body as though she was about to be
tortured. Her heart was pounding in her ears so
loudly she was aware of nothing save that she was

there in his arms, trapped and unable to get away.

'David, don't!' She moaned his name softly.

'I'll be very gentle with you.' He held her and kissed her so deeply her body was forced into a response. She seemed to yield compulsively and his imperious hands moved over her hungrily, cupping her tender breasts, shifting the filmy material aside so he could find her warm, satin flesh.

She was going, going, losing herself in sensation. There was no longer any need for him to hold her head, because it had fallen back weakly against his shoulder, her soft mouth opened as though she craved what she tried hardest to deny.

'Marry me,' his voice called her back from wherever she had gone.

'You don't love me.'

'You damned little fool!'

It was different now, the lovemaking, not so controlled or so infinitely patient. He kissed her then, caressed her, as if he had become addicted to a sweetness he despised. It was ravishing, instant wanting, but it wasn't love. There was no tenderness behind it, but a tremendously controlled violence. Another minute and he would take her, and she couldn't possibly change any of it.

'Stop me,' he muttered harshly, and twined his hand through her silky hair.

'What can I say?' She could feel the trembling in his strong arms. 'You knew exactly how this would be.'

'I'm sorry. I thought you knew about my obsession.' Abruptly he lifted her away from him so she fell full length on the sofa.

'I want you, Catherine, until it comes to the point. Man has always been the aggressor and I'm all in favour of winning, but at the moment I can't imagine raping the woman I intend to marry.'

'You mean you're not really just selfish?'

'I don't suppose I ever have been.' He turned to look down at her, the moonlight making fascinating patterns on her gracefully relaxed body.

'Surely you've forgotten all about Christine?' she said a little savagely.

'What about her?' He sat down again so she had to move right back to look at him.

'I take it she welcomed your every advance?'

'I've never slept with her, if that's what you're asking.'

'Forgive me, she told me you did!' She was starting to get excited, lifting herself up so she was looking right in to his face.

'And you believed her?' he asked curtly.

'What else could I do?' She shrugged her delicate shoulders. 'I mean, what was to stop you?'

'It's odd *you* should ask that. It isn't all that easy to sleep with a woman one doesn't find attractive.'

'Are you trying to tell me you don't find me attractive?' He might have struck her she was so shocked.

'I thought we were talking about Christine,' he said, very gently.

'But of course!' Catherine couldn't help the little sigh of relief. 'Why do you really want to marry me?'

'I know exactly what I'm doing,' he said deliberately.

'With no gain?' She wanted to hurt him, so she said it bitterly.

She saw the tautness come into his face and his eyes narrowed. 'After all, Catherine, you don't know me very well. I can quite see that now.'

'Well, do you still want me?' A strange trembling ran through her and unconsciously she held her breath.

'Yes,' he said curtly, 'I do.'

CHAPTER SEVEN

SYDNEY she loved; the magnificent harbour with its innumerable coves and bays, its big, bustling excitement. After life in the North, there was always a frenzy of movement around her, and this, more than anything, reawakened her to life.

Aunt Edith had a perfectly beautiful, smallish house standing proudly on a cliff overlooking the fabulously blue water and she lost no time in drawing up an itinerary to ensure that Catherine would see all the sights the city had to offer. By day they went on trips and at night they saw plays and concerts and ballet and even two important antique auctions because Aunt Edith was a collector and her accumulated treasures spread right through the house.

Into all this she had drawn her three nephews and her niece. Aunt Edith was a spinster because, as she said, her father had never considered anyone good enough for her, but despite this she had considerable skill in handling young people and under-

standing their problems. Catherine went everywhere, sometimes with her and sometimes with her
ever-lively young relations, and gradually she lost
her look of soft melancholy and began to take interest in everything that was going on around her.

The weeks slipped into months and with her return to good physical and mental health Catherine
discovered something significant was missing from
her life. It struck her forcibly more and more each
day. She was having a good time, swimming and
sailing and partying and accompanying Aunt Edith
around all the art galleries and antique shops, but
all the wonderful things she was seeing and doing
left an empty space that occasionally made her feel
peculiar.

She wanted to see David; to feel his hateful magic.
Why didn't he ring or write or even come to see
her? Of course he was busy and something was always happening that required his attention, but
still, *months*? She didn't understand herself, and
though she went to a lot of parties and seemed to
attract a lot of gratifying attention, she was not the
least fascinated by anyone. She even found herself
examining faces trying to see a resemblance to
David. It was ridiculous. No one had his dark, force-
ful good looks, his black hair and his gleaming
golden eyes. No one was even as tall, or had his
splendid physique and unique way of moving. No
one reminded her of a golden puma at all. Brett
came the closest, and Brett was David's cousin, not
yet through Architecture at the Sydney University.

Brett was fun and very attractive and she clung
to him a little because he reminded her of David.

She could see that now, although it took Aunt Edith to point it out to her. The others were a little jealous, Peter and Ian, but then they were blond and seemed much too young. It was odd to miss a man one had run away from, worse to know he seemed bent on ignoring her. Here, she was much sought after and confident because of it, so it was all the more frightening not knowing what David wanted of her. To all intents and purposes she hadn't existed for months.

Spring turned to summer and now Catherine began to talk about getting a job.

'What kind of a job, dear?' Aunt Edith put down her antique catalogue to ask vaguely.

'Where's David?' she asked with a kind of frustration. 'This has gone on long enough.'

'I thought you were enjoying yourself?' Aunt Edith's dark eyes widened behind her glasses.

'I am!' Catherine swung around in quick contrition. 'I've never had such a wonderful time in my life, but. . . .'

'Don't tell me, let me guess. You've been working up to this for some time. You want David to come and take you away.'

'No.' She wasn't pretending the fright.

'I don't understand,' Aunt Edith said abruptly. 'I take it you two are still going to get married.'

'I wish I knew,' Catherine laughed oddly.

'Well, you're beautiful and intelligent. . . .'

'That's nothing,' Catherine interrupted.

'And you've got lots of character. Please let me finish. Would you like me to ring him?'

'Don't be mad!' protested Catherine.

'It's just nerves.' Aunt Edith shook her head. 'Didn't you tell me you were going out tonight.'

'I'd almost forgotten.'

'I see.' Aunt Edith went back to her catalogue dryly and they both laughed.

'You've been so good to me. *For* me,' Catherine said for what had to be the umpteenth time. 'I just wish I knew some way to repay you.'

'You've done that by turning my rather lonely life into a whirl of pleasure,' Aunt Edith smiled slightly. 'I've told you before, I was absolutely delighted to have you and I'd like to have your company for ever.'

'How nice you are!' Catherine came over and kissed the older woman's cheek with spontaneous affection. 'I've never had an aunty.'

'You've got one now.'

At the weekend, she and Brett went off to the races to see some of the top thoroughbreds in the country before they contested the Melbourne Cup in a few weeks' time. Neither of them were enthusiastic gamblers, Catherine more daring than Brett, yet they still managed to come home a little richer purely through following the favourites. They left early, before the last race, to avoid the crowds, and not surprisingly considering their penchant for one another, argued amicably about what they would do that night. They were still arguing when they arrived back at Aunt Edith's and there all arguments came to an end.

They could hear Aunt Edith laughing before they ever found their way out to the rear patio, lush with green foliage and blooming flowers and the most magnificent view, but even then they didn't suspect who it was. Brett saw him first, and he rushed forward like an eager schoolboy, passing his hand over his dazzled eyes.

'Dave, you beauty!'

'Brett!' He stood up smilingly, turning to face them and shaking his cousin's hand. 'Good to see you, and how you've grown!'

'I doubt if I'll be your height,' Brett said happily. 'Just wait until Mum knows you're in town!'

'I've already spoken to her.' David moved towards Catherine and looked down at her with his curiously brilliant eyes. 'How are you, Catherine?'

'Fine.' Of course she lifted her face, not knowing what else to do, and he bent his head and brushed her cheek.

'I think I like the new hair-do,' he told her.

'Liz took me along to her hairdresser.' Liz was Brett's sister and they had become very friendly.

'Obviously he knows his stuff.' Brett looked at Catherine with pride. 'I hope you don't mind my taking Cathy with me everywhere?'

'It's very nice of you, Brett.' David gave his cousin a lazy smile.

'I suppose now you're going to fire me?'

'That's it,' David said suavely, 'and thank you very much.'

'Well, come on, you two, sit down and have a cool drink,' Aunt Edith ordered. 'I suppose you did lose your money?'

'Thank you very much, but we won!' Brett didn't hesitate for a moment. He was very thirsty. 'Tell us, Dave, when did you arrive?'

'About ten minutes after you left.'

'What a ghastly piece of luck!' Brett tipped his chair back to a dangerous angle. 'Of course Cathy has been pining for you dreadfully.'

Catherine flushed and accepted her drink. 'That sounds as if I've been dull company.'

'Sweetie,' Brett shook his head, 'you're the best company I know. Dave is a lucky man. I don't mind telling you if it hadn't been Dave I would probably have made a fool of myself.'

'Strictly speaking this should be champagne for a celebration,' Aunt Edith said smilingly. With her cheeks flushed and her eyes shining, she looked very handsome indeed.

'Never mind, we'll have it tonight.' David glanced briefly at Catherine. Her face was in profile and she looked very chic and beautiful. 'Do you know who you reminded me of, Brett, when you came through that door?'

'No.' Brett sat up, madly stimulated by his cousin's sudden appearance.

'Me.'

'Of course you're right!' said Brett, highly flattered. 'Mum always said I took after you.'

By the time Catherine reached her room she was trembling all over. He was here, and the whole heartbreaking business would start over again. There had to be an answer and she would have to look for it. She couldn't possibly marry him, though she had committed herself shockingly. She went to the window and began to rock herself back and forth violently. There was a price for everything, and now he had come to claim her. Whatever his reasons, she could be sure it wasn't love. Did a lover never ring or write or show more interest in his cousin? When she threw up her head, there were tears on her cheeks.

They had dinner where it cost a fortune and she wore one of her prettiest dresses, a strapless champagne silk that made the most of her beautiful, gilded skin. She didn't know what David expected, but certainly not this silence. She couldn't seem to get a thing out. The world was full of beautiful, intelligent women who knew how to make conversation, so how had she earned herself the privilege of sitting opposite him? His was a strong, disturbing personality and now she could see more clearly, she couldn't match him in any way.

Afterwards he just seemed to want to drive, but finally they pulled up with a view of the ocean and the sound of the surf crashing on the sand. He was driving Aunt Edith's big old Daimler and in the dim light from the panel she could see the arrogant cast of his face.

'Relax, Catherine, I'm not going to touch you.'

It was only then she realised she had been holding her breath. 'Let's go for a walk,' she said.

'In those sandals?' He glanced downwards, but he couldn't actually see her gold evening sandals.

'I'll take them off.'

'Then you'd better wait until we get down to the beach.' He opened his door and came round to her.

The salt breeze was blowing and it whipped at her hair, skeining it across his jacket. 'Now you're here, I don't know what to say to you,' she sighed.

'That's obvious,' he said dryly. 'At least it's better than a desolate little face. You may not be able to find your tongue, but you've gained a great deal.'

'In what way?' Her head tilted high.

'Oh, if possible, you're more beautiful.' His gleaming eyes travelled over her small slender figure.

'You mean you've allowed me so much money I can buy the right clothes.'

'Actually the differences are more subtle than that. I'm glad Brett had the good sense to stop short of falling in love with you.'

'I guess like the rest of us he goes in awe of you.'

They had reached the beach and as she leant back on a rock he bent down and slipped off her sandals, putting them in the pocket of his jacket. 'You want to walk, let's walk.'

The moon clearly illuminated both of them. It was an enchanting night and a strong gust of wind drove straight in from the pounding surf. Up on the cliffs, the light poured out of the houses and they could hear the sound of music. Someone playing their stereo equipment, for the quality of the sound filled the night with a love song. Catherine tried to put it out of her mind, though she knew the words well.

Feelings, nothing more than feelings....

The song always moved her to tenderness, now it filled her with a speechless craving.

'Hadn't you better take it a little slower?' David grasped her arm and made her fall back a step.

'I can't marry you, David,' she said so baldly it staggered her.

'A pity, when I haven't the slightest intention of letting you get away.'

'But why? You can't expect me to believe in love any more?'

'But that's not why you're marrying me.' He dropped his hands on her shoulders and turned her to look at him. 'Isn't it because you can't stand being on your own? Add to that, I can give you all you've missed in your life. You need me and you know it!'

'I only know that I can't ... can't....' her little whisper trailed away.

'Sleep with me?'

'Please understand, David,' she begged.

'Oh, I do.' He bent and touched her mouth lightly. 'That's the last kiss you'll be getting until you come to me of your own accord.'

'Do you mean it?' She didn't realise it, but she was holding fast to his fingers.

'I've promised, haven't I? It's an empty form of marriage, but believe me I'll ask nothing of you unless you want it.'

'Promise me again.' She leaned forward like a child and pressed her head against his chest.

'God!' he said softly, and pulled her fully into the circle of his arms. 'Marriage with a child like you, but you'll never get away.'

Their marriage was one of the biggest the North had ever seen. There were hundreds of guests. They came from inter-State, and overseas, and because of her intense nervousness Catherine didn't know she looked miraculously beautiful in her satin wedding gown, drawing breaths of admiration when she

threw back her wedding veil to reveal her face. Her
eyes were shining with an unearthly radiance and
no one questioned or hesitated over the reason. She
was a beloved bride. Only two people knew differ-
ently, and how could they keep from hurting each
other?

The reception was held at the house, but Catherine hardly remembered a moment of it. She was
utterly bemused and shaken by the church cere-
mony. It was one thing to plan a marriage in cold
blood and another to answer one's vows. Marriage
was a consecration, or it should be.

Later she stood in the bedroom she had used before she had gone away and changed into her travelling clothes. When they came back, she would be
using the master bedroom, and already a lot of her
things had been moved into it. She hadn't asked
where her husband would be sleeping.

Her husband. Yet there would be little difference
in their relationship. Bridegrooms were usually
nervous, but *his* self-assurance was unassailable. It
had to be so, and he was giving nothing of himself
away.

Their honeymoon lasted three weeks because of
business commitments and in that time David
underwent a personality change; treating her like a
slightly moody, mostly charming younger sister who
had to be humoured and indulged at every turn.
Only occasionally did she turn to find him watching
her, and those moments were so wildly unsettling
she was grateful they happened rarely.

From New Zealand, they had flown to Hawaii,

and its tropical beauty and colourful way of life reminded her of home. Even the State flower, the hibiscus, grew no more prolifically here than it did in tropical Queensland and the people had the same love of informality and gaily patterned clothes. The major crop, sugar, was the same, and one night they had dinner with the head of a corporation that owned one of the largest plantations in the islands. The next day, while Catherine went shopping, the same man took David off on a tour of corporation interests including a pineapple plantation and a processing plant, and as these too were Hungerford interests they got on extremely well.

In this time, Catherine had been prepared for a good deal of verbal sparring by day and sheer panic at night, but while David danced attendance on her, his attitude couldn't remotely have been described as lover-like. Her trousseau was beautiful, her exquisite night clothes, but David scarcely glanced at her in their bedroom and he was always up first and the last to retire. She hadn't even received a chaste kiss on the forehead, so she was forced to accept that he meant to keep his part of the bargain. After all, he was a highly civilised man, for the most part. She had decided to put the odd, all-engulfing glance at the back of her mind, though at the time it rang like a warning bell.

The first week they were back, the invitations poured in, including one from Mr and Mrs Athol Somers. This triggered off a mild temper tantrum because Mrs Somers was none other than Christine, but David only turned on her firmly.

'I suppose you know we do business?' he told her, hunting up a tie.

'Even so, I thought—*Christine!*' One part of her mind was registering his dark attraction, the other disturbed by the idea of meeting Christine again.

'Grow up, baby,' he said lightly. 'They're probably very happy. Like us.'

In the end they went along to the Somers' dinner party. There were four other couples beside themselves, all pleasant, obviously well-to-do people, but none so young as Catherine. Athol Somers was the surprise, and unable to help herself, Catherine stared at him with wide open eyes. He was short, at least an half a head shorter than his bride, barrel-chested, with an almost featureless face and a totally bald pate. What was even more surprising, Catherine liked him. He took her extended hand very gently as if anxious he might hurt so delicate a creature and smiled directly into her eyes. Close up, his eyes were his best feature, small, but very bright and shrewd.

'Delighted to meet you, my dear.' He was moving his big head up and down in approval. 'I truly mean that. You sure are beautiful, little lady.'

'Thank you.'

Christine was smiling, her fair lashes, heavily mascaraed, fluttering at David. She seemed heavier and her svelte body was rather generously displayed. 'I'm extremely sorry we had to miss the wedding, Dave.'

'Oh well, we had one of our own!' Athol Somers gave a great shout of laughter and looked around for rapport. He was what is known as a 'rough diamond', but so tough and rich he was insensible to the opinions of those who found him crude and overpowering. At least he was deeply in love with his wife, and from the telling look on his face it seemed certain Christine wasn't witholding her favours. Athol Somers didn't look like a man who would stand for it anyway, and if everyone in the town had already concluded he had bought his handsome bride, it was obvious, so far, that he wasn't regretting the deal.

The house, a mansion that had once belonged to one of the old 'sugar' families, Athol had completely restored. Unfortunately the decorators had been harassed by his taste and the result was all flaming carpets, bright colours and a large quota of very expensive but inelegant furniture and light fittings.

The Japanese couple, visitors from Tokyo, whose own home was an aesthetic triumph, were infinitely compassionate about showing their dismay, but the Italian business tycoon made a dramatic gesture with his hands that Catherine interpreted as it was all too dreadful.

Dinner, however, was superb. Athol had a splendid appetite and food to him was as desirable as money. Under his influence, Christine appeared to be forgetting her diet, for she ate far too much to keep herself in great shape. One had only to admire her skill as a hostess, however. She was very well informed about her guests' work and interests and she had an uncanny ability to smooth over her husband's rough bits and make him appear funny.

Afterwards, when the men began to talk business, she momentarily drew Catherine aside. 'So you did it after all?' Throwing a backward beaming look at the other ladies she took hold of Catherine's arm, lifting her voice. 'My dear, I simply have to show you our wedding present. We got one, yes indeed!'

Of course all the charm and vitality had merely been an act, for now it was completely washed from her face. She looked tiger-toothed and as hard as nails, and she led Catherine through the house to the master bedroom. There, without warning, she closed the door and leaned against it, her breathing moving the lace over her full bosom.

'Well now,' she muttered, 'what does it feel like to be married to Dave?'

'Why does it worry you?' Catherine managed a smile. 'You must have everything you want.'

'Definitely not love!' She stared at Catherine with something very close to hatred.

'But your husband loves you.'

'Probably it's something to do with gratitude. Athol has it, even if it's well hidden.'

'I like him.' Catherine was disconcerted by the open contempt in the other woman's eyes. Obviously Christine could have considered the stage. Athol Somers was far from being a fool, yet he believed his wife had a genuine feeling for him.

'How nice!' Christine said bitterly. 'But then you're a very nice little girl.'

'Shouldn't we go back to the others?' Catherine nearly shuddered at the purple drapes.

'Wait. We do have a present for you—Athol bought it.' Christine walked to the louvred wall of cupboards and took a box down from an upper shelf. 'A very magnanimous man is Athol, and of course he admires Dave immensely. Needs him too if this oil exploration thing is to go through.'

'I didn't know.' Catherine looked down at the box on the bed.

'Why would you?' Christine's face kindled with a quick anger. 'You're unaware of anything Dave does. All you know is your silly little self and how you've been victimised by life. You know why he married you, of course? Pity. The strong are often like that. They lend their strength to the weak. But you're not really married to him, darling, are you?' She suddenly reached out and grasped Catherine's chin, holding her face ruthlessly to the light. 'Oh yes, you've got his name, and you think you have him tied, but I don't think you're giving him much satisfaction in bed. In fact, I don't think you're in his bed at all.'

'At least you never were!' Catherine stared at her.

'My God, what an innocent!' Christine's coarse laugh challenged her. 'You know as well as I do Dave has made love to me—more times than I can ever remember, more times than I care to forget. There's no one like Dave. All the time, while I suffer Athol, I make believe it's Dave. And I *do* suffer,' she added slowly, a peculiar light in her pale blue eyes.

'I'm sorry,' Catherine said simply, and pulled away. 'But I didn't deprive you of David, you know. Whatever you may think, it was David who wanted me.'

'You know I can't have a child?'

'I'm sorry,' Catherine repeated, feeling numb.

'Every man wants a son.'

'All my life I've known that.' A little sob escaped from Catherine's throat.

'You're such a fool, aren't you?' Christine looked at her with terrible eyes. 'The only thing you can do for Dave is give him a child, but I expect you cringe every time he comes near you. You have a very virginal look for a bride.'

'Don't brood on it, that may all change tonight,' Catherine said, trying to make her voice hard. 'I really think we should go back. This isn't getting either of us anywhere.'

'No?' Christine challenged her, her colour high. 'You've told me all I wanted to know.'

Catherine went to walk to the door and Christine gave a high, triumphant laugh and whipped the lid off the cardboard box.

'You haven't seen your wedding present.'

'I don't think I care to.'

'Don't offend Athol,' Christine warned jeeringly. 'Dave wouldn't like that.'

'I think I know David a little more than you do,' Catherine said with quiet dignity, though she was filled with a deep sense of inadequacy. She turned her beautifully shaped curly head over her shoulder and looked down at massive silver tureen.

'It cost a pretty penny!' Christine drawled. 'Antique, of course. He knows Dave is used to the best.'

Catherine knew her husband wouldn't like the design any more than she did, but she murmured sincerely, 'That was very kind of him.'

'Of course he's got appalling taste, but I couldn't tell him. He's like a child.'

'Chrissy?'

A strong voice was calling outside the door and when Christine threw it open, her husband looked at her indulgently, then engulfed her in a bear hug. 'Ah, so you've been showing Catherine our wedding present?'

'It's beautiful, Mr Somers!' Catherine offered gravely.

'Athol, please, as we're going to be friends.'

Christine's expression at that moment was that she couldn't endure it, but fortunately her husband was beaming at their guest. She was wearing an expensive slip of a dress in a deep shade of gold and Athol found himself thinking David Hungerford had got himself one heck of a beautiful little wife.

Catherine was almost silent going home and when they arrived, she found she had a headache.

'I'll go up to bed now, David, if you don't mind.'

'You've lost colour,' he commented.

'I have a headache.'

'You've been getting a few too many of them, haven't you?' he asked dryly.

'Well, you won't let me do anything.'

'Be reasonable, Catherine,' he walked to the bedroom door. 'I can't let you work.'

'No, I'm your child bride in a castle.' She couldn't blot out the things Christine had said.

'Do you want me to tell you about the business?'

'Yes.' She picked up a hairbrush and ran it through her glossy mass of hair.

'All right, then, I will. After all, I'll do anything to make you my rightful wife.'

There was a mocking undertone to his vibrant voice and as she looked across at him, something stirred in her, some terrible sweep of emotion that was reflected in her eyes.

'Do you like children, David?' she asked abruptly.

'I like you.' He looked back at her steadily and there was a flame in his golden eyes.

'I don't think I can bear this,' she said, in a husky emotional voice.

'Neither do I for very much longer!' His tone was perfectly hard, far removed from loving.

'It's not working, is it?' she asked in a hushed voice.

'Listen, flower face, I'm going to say goodnight.' David half turned his lean, powerful body away. 'I've got rather a busy day tomorrow.'

Her whole body flushed crimson as though he had struck her. 'I expect you'll be gone before I get up?'

He knew that he had hurt her, but he didn't seem to care. 'Don't worry, I always look in on you. You look sad, even when you're asleep.'

He turned then and walked away from her, leaving her to the quiet sanctuary of the huge double bed.

The days slipped by slowly and Catherine couldn't even trust herself to be alone with her husband. Often she wished to heaven she could go back to her old state where nothing seemed to matter, for now her heart was full of the deepest, most humiliating emotions. Now when she craved physical fulfilment, so desperate sometimes she could hardly breathe, her husband didn't happen to want her any more. If he ever had. Even when he had brought her home the most adorable little puppy he had only briefly touched her cheek. In that moment he could have had anything from her, but he had only moved off abruptly and reached for a cigarette.

Then, one Saturday morning, when David went out to buy a piece of property, Catherine dressed quickly and went over to the farm. It was the first time she had ever gone back and she didn't know why she was going now, except that she had to. The property was still hers because she didn't want to sell it, but one day she would have to let it go.

It still hurt her. Everything still hurt her. She wandered through the rooms reliving the past. Such sorrow had disturbed her life, perhaps in a sense making her neurotic. Her father's clothing had been taken away and the house was hushed and secret.

In the dining room she paused and ran her hands lovingly over her mother's dining room suite. She was far more knowledgeable now about antiques, and she decided there and then that she would polish it. Of course there was no room for it up at the house, but she would have it stored as she couldn't bear to part with it.

An hour slipped by and after she had washed up she sat down in a lounge chair and tried to think about her life. She should never have married David. She had given away her soul. Tears trickled out of her eyes, and she got up and stretched out on the sofa. She hadn't been sleeping at all well, for as soon as she closed her eyes she drifted into dreams of David—wild, unhappy dreams, where she felt the lash of his anger. Once she dreamt he had taken her with a fierce passion and in the morning she couldn't look at him for fear of betraying herself with flushed cheeks. Christine, too, came into her dreams. Christine with her cruel, malicious tongue. She knew well how to feed poison to others.

She was half in and half out of an unhappy, drugged state when she heard the sound of a car door slam. Disorientated, she sat up quickly and brushed the tears from her eyes. There was a small stain on her yellow and white sundress and she had the irresistible urge to hide. Who would come here, unless it was David, and he was twenty miles away.

How silly, how stupid it was to be caught with tear streaks on her cheeks. She wasn't mistress of herself at all, but the sad child David had called her.

Then he was calling her, and she sprang to her feet in shock. She tried to hide so much from him, she started back when he came through the house to confront her.

'What the devil are you doing here?' He spoke with controlled harshness, and even in her passion of embarrassment she could see how disturbed he was.

'I just thought it was time I came over,' she explained.

'You've been crying.'

'Yes.' She brought up her hand to brush her heavy eyelashes. 'I just wanted to be alone.'

'And have me half out of my mind?' His eyes were a golden blaze, annihilating her.

'Why?' He had crossed the floor, towering over her, and all at once the air in the room was so oppressive she couldn't breathe.

'You don't believe I worry about you?'

She shook her head quickly, knowing she was

goading him, but unable to stop.

'Well, I do, all the time.'

There were shadows beneath her eyes, emerald green and full of pain.

'Don't cry,' he said curtly as those same eyes filled with crystalline tears.

'I can't help it.' She put up her two hands and covered her face.

'*Catherine!*' She could hear his hard breathing, then he pulled her into his arms. 'Don't cry, I can't stand it.'

'That's wonderful!' Her voice rose to a cry. 'What *am* I to you?' She lifted her head with such passion her whole body shook. 'A lost child? A kid sister?'

'Whatever you are, if you don't stop I'll make love to you until you're screaming for mercy.'

'But you promised!' She was sobbing in her extremity.

'I was a damn fool!' He sounded utterly ruthless. 'I want to devour you!'

Though she cried out against it, he swooped and swung her up into his steely arms, walking through with her to her old bedroom.

Her narrow single bed was still there against the wall, and he threw her down on it and joined her, turning her in to his lean, powerful body.

'Remember me? I'm your husband.'

'No, David.' She put her hand pleadingly on his arm, but something very strange was happening to her. She was dissolving, going weightless, warmed by the exultant golden light that poured from his eyes.

He moved, and his body was a weighted ravishment. She wanted it to crush her. Yet he made no move to kiss her but slipped his hand over her breast so the dusky nipple sprang to life against his palm.

'Aren't you going to fight me?' There was a torrent of passion in him, swift and molten.

'No, it's all over.'

She lay there with the hot tears stinging her eyes and her body breaking to rapture. The sun was streaming through the window, the air perfumed with the mixed scents of the garden, fruit and flower.

She didn't know how she was going to survive what was about to happen. It all seemed so shockingly erotic in broad daylight, there on the bed she had slept in ever since she was a little girl.

With his hands caressing her breasts she was filled with such ecstasy she began to make soft little moaning sounds, exciting to the male, but still he didn't kiss her, but held off, looking down at her perfect, gleaming skin and her huge, tormented eyes.

'How beautiful you are, Catherine,' he said quietly. 'I'll always remember how you look at this moment.'

She didn't answer, but her beautiful eyes filled with tears. Somehow the bodice of her dress had slipped away and when he slid his hands down over her narrow, taut hips, she could feel the contractions start deep in the pit of her stomach, remorseless and insistent.

'I'm afraid.'

'Don't be.'

His hands lingered, stirring her to full life, teasing her until she could have cried aloud. Every part of her body was aware of him, frantic with wanting.

Never in her life had she experienced such a fierce, driving desire.

'Catherine?' He turned her face around. 'Do you love me?'

She wanted to cry, 'Beyond anything!' but the words wouldn't come. Only her lips moved and with a muffled exclamation he caught her parted mouth and explored it so passionately she began to move feverishly right into his arms, something she had never done, but the wanting was too strong.

'Look at me,' he said.

Her eyes had been tightly closed, but at the curt command they flew open.

'In another moment you'll lose the right to stop me.'

'I don't ... want ... to!' She felt drugged with desire.

A shudder went right through his strong body and he lifted her over him, unable to subdue his own turbulent emotions. This was his wife and there was no escape for her now.

After that, he made love to her all the time; night, morning, mindless rapture, and just when she began to feel safe, even loved, something happened to cut through the shimmering veils of illusion.

She had seen Jon from time to time, since the wedding, never alone, so when he rang one day and asked her to lunch she found it impossible to say no. After all, he was her friend of a lifetime and it would be pleasant to sit down and just gossip. Her position as Mrs David Hungerford allowed no time for that. Indeed, it had cut her off a good deal from her old circle of friends. They were all young and in very ordinary circumstances, and she sometimes missed the old irreverent chit-chat. Very few of David's friends and business associates had the time to sit around a coffee shop and listen to Renzo strumming his guitar, even if they had the inclination.

When she met Jon inside Angelo's, he pressed her hand in gratitude, then leaned forward and kissed her cheek. 'Thanks for coming,' he said.

'Why wouldn't I have lunch with my oldest friends?' She smiled at him and sat down in her chair.

'You look ... different.' Jon was gazing at her intensely. 'Very chic and expensive.'

'You don't like it?' She was a little amused at his tone.

'I don't think you're my Cathy any more.'

'Yes, I am.' She was concerned at the unhappiness in his eyes. 'Let's order.'

They didn't speak until the waitress had gone away, then Jon said apologetically, 'I suppose I shouldn't have brought you here.'

'Why ever not?' Catherine looked at him in surprise.

'It's not good enough, that's why. I don't imagine your husband even knows it exists.'

'Oh, I think so,' Catherine's tone was dry. 'There's not much he doesn't know about.'

Jon didn't speak for several moments, then he said sombrely, 'Are you happy?'

'Why, yes!' Catherine tried to smile. 'What is it, Jon? You look ... tired.'

'You know what's the matter with me,' he uttered, very quietly. 'At night I imagine you up there with him.'

'Please, Jon!' She looked at him in distress.

'I still love you, Cathy,' he spoke with painful difficulty. 'I guess I always will.'

'But I'm married, Jon.' She was vaguely startled at the depths of his intensity. 'Remember, you came to the wedding.'

'It was the worst day of my life.'

'I'm sorry.' She reached out and took his hand. 'You're the last person I'd ever want to hurt.'

'Because of Patrick? Because we were all friends?'

'Because of you,' she said compassionately, and sought to change the subject. 'How's your mother?'

'The same. Mother doesn't change.' He was looking down at their locked hands. 'Mother did a lot to ruin it for me, with you.'

'That's not true!' Catherine said firmly, but she couldn't ease her hand away. 'Your mother loves you, Jon. Please don't turn away from her now. You don't know how lucky you are, just having a parent.'

'I don't see that at all.' Jon's thin face went grim. 'She wanted to break us up and she did.'

'Oh, Jon.' Catherine sat very quietly, waiting for him to release her hand, but he didn't. 'You've always been such a fair person. You're not being fair now.'

'Tell me you've made a mistake, Cathy.'

'About what?' There was a film of emotion across his eyes that worried her.

'Your marriage. You've never known a man like David Hungerford.'

'No, I never have,' she said simply. 'Please let go of my hand, Jon. It's going numb.'

'I'm sorry.' He drew a quick breath and his fingers unclenched. 'You're so young and innocent, and I find his behaviour contemptible.'

'I don't understand you.' Catherine's face whitened at the vitriolic charge.

'I'm sorry, I shouldn't have spoken.' Jon shook his head, a little dazedly. 'They say the wives are the last to know.'

Catherine detested herself for starting to shake. 'Having gone so far, Jon, please explain yourself.'

'It's just this.' He was looking very emotional. 'He's got you, the most beautiful girl in this whole damned world, yet he still hangs on to his discarded mistress.'

'*No!*' More than anything in the world, Catherine didn't want to believe it.

'I'm afraid he does.' Jon's mouth thinned with contempt. 'He isn't like the rest of us, you know. He can do what he damned well likes.'

'No.' Catherine forced herself to sit still in the chair. She wanted to run and hide, but she knew she had to face this like a mature woman. 'I don't believe it, Jon. Someone is out to destroy his reputation. Maybe this woman you're hinting about.'

'Christine Somers, of course. God, Cathy, do you need any more verification? They've been linked together for years.'

'He didn't marry her,' Catherine pointed out, low-voiced.

'Then you can bet your life he had a good reason.'

Yes, he wanted a son. A man always wanted a son.

'I hate to hurt you, Cathy,' Jon clasped his hands together until his knuckles showed white, his haggard young face showing real emotion. 'Leave him. You can—everyone gets divorced these days.'

'*I* don't.' Catherine looked down at the magnificent emerald and diamond ring on her finger. It was exquisite, but not important like her gold wedding band.

'He took advantage of you, you know,' Jon said intensely. 'He never gave you time to recover. He just swept you off your feet with all his rotten money.'

'I wouldn't care if he never had a penny.' Catherine stood up. 'I'm very sorry, Jon, but I've lost my appetite.'

Jon stood up, too, much agitated, clutching the table. 'God, Cathy, don't go.'

'I must.' She looked at his face which looked so strained and hopeless. 'I would never, ever, suspect you, Jon, of lying to me.'

'I'm not!' He stared at her, looking as though he were about to cry. 'I had to tell you, Cathy. You must see that. You're so inexperienced, and he's not good enough for you.'

'Goodbye.'

'No.' Jon flung a handful of notes down on to the table and grasped her arm. 'I don't want anything either.'

The waitress, coming back with their pasta, looked her astonishment, then shrugged when she saw the notes on the table. She was new in the town, so she took it for a lovers' spat.

Others, however, were aware that the beautiful

young woman was Mrs David Hungerford and the young man who held her hand and accompanied her out with such shamefully apparent emotion was Jon Morley, a Hungerford employee. One of these was Mrs Christine Somers' maid, and she couldn't wait to tell her mistress just how much undesirable attention the young Mrs Hungerford had called to herself. In her position she could have been expected to act more properly.

That afternoon Catherine just drove around aimlessly with Prince, her adorable little collie pup, to keep her company. At the lake she got out and sat watching the myriad reflections of the sun on the water. In the shade, the water was as still and deeply green as the ring on her finger.

It was hard to think of the man one loved so desperately making love to another woman—a bitter, devastating, mortification. Just when she had rejected Christine's malicious claims, Jon had confirmed them, and Jon would never lie to her. He was her friend.

The little dog could hardly believe she wanted to sit down, staring so vacantly, so he tugged at her shoe and she smiled at him because he was so alive and so beautiful. David loved him too, and often they stood side by side just looking at his antics. A gift of love. Catherine had wanted so desperately to believe that.

The grass on the far side of the lake was getting very long and she called Prince out of it. There were always snakes about, mostly harmless, but she wasn't taking chances with her little friend.

'Here, Prince—here, boy!' She really would have to start to train him. Collies were so intelligent he would soon learn to obey her. Even if the marriage broke up, she would still have her dog. A little laugh broke from her, contorting her face.

'Prince, where are you, boy?' He must have scampered into the long grass and she looked down at the useless lead in her hand. Freedom. Everyone wanted freedom. Was there any?

The grass rustled and as she turned, there was the pup.

'Come to Mamma!' she called.

The puppy crouched, its tail wagging, then off it went again, longing for a game.

Rainbow-hued parrots flew out of the stately trees and over the deep end of the pool, and as Catherine looked up at them she took a step forward and immediately recoiled in shock. Something had stung her ankle and as she looked down she saw a snake slip away with stealthy speed. In all her life she had never been bitten by a snake, so it didn't seem possible.

The puppy, strangely enough, ran back to her as though it knew something had happened, and as she dragged herself back to the car it set up the funniest howling.

'I'm all right, boy!'

But she knew she wasn't. Her thoughts ranged swiftly over all her accumulated knowledge of snakebite. She certainly couldn't identify the snake. It had disappeared in a flash, a sombre dark colour. Many years ago in her childhood a neighbour had been bitten by a taipan and had died. These days they had antidotes if only one could get to a hospital.

She slid her shoe off and looked down at her ankle. There they were, the puncture marks. All she had to do now was stop the poison moving. She didn't know she was gasping, but the little dog had its head on the side, ears cocked. She hadn't as yet felt the impact of fear. It wasn't a taipan, it wasn't long enough and it lacked the taipan's rich colouring. Probably, had it been, she might have been dead by now. The taipan was the most feared snake in Australia, among the deadliest in the world.

What could she use for a tourniquet, or didn't they use a tourniquet any more? The things one ought to know and didn't! Sweat had broken out on her head and she felt sick and clammy. Even as she bent to tie the lead tightly above the wound, she pitched forward dizzily. No one would find her and she wasn't capable of driving the car. Prince was whimpering, running under her arm and getting right into her face. There he settled and there he stayed, until they found her.

She was very sick for two days and all that time her husband scarcely left her bedside. It was he who had found her, along with the local police officer who hunted up the snake and killed it. It was one of the family of black snakes and once it was identified the information was radioed in to the hospital so the anti-venin was ready when Catherine was rushed in; a high speed chase that she knew nothing about and beyond the limits of an ordinary car.

On the third day she was allowed home, but David insisted she spend the rest of the day in bed. This she did, although she insisted the puppy be brought in for a while, where it curled up on her bed. Both of them slept, and when she opened her eyes again it was night.

'How are you feeling.' Her husband came to the bedside, looking down at her with searching eyes.

'Hungry, I think.'

'That's good.' He smiled at her and laid his hand along her cheek. 'Anything special you fancy?'

'Just you.'

She didn't know why she said that, it just came out.

'Well, you've got me,' he said briefly. 'I'll go away and see about getting you something to eat.'

'Have you had anything?' she called after him. Always lean, he looked thinner—fine-drawn, taut.

'No.'

'Have it with me?'

'All right.' He smiled and his dark face lightened, his teeth white against his deep tan.

Primo cooked them a delicious chicken dish and Lee set it up in their bedroom. The entire household had been greatly upset over the past few days and relief turned everything into a festive mood. Lee had even found the time to make a little floral arrangement and he bowed and smiled in a manner that was positively exuberant for him, then left the room.

'I'll get up,' said Catherine, 'if you'll pass me my robe.'

It matched her nightgown, part of her exquisite trousseau, and David held it for her while she slipped her arms into it.

They ate in a companionable near-silence. David

seemed preoccupied, and afterwards he took the tray down into the kitchen. While he was gone, Catherine washed her face, brushed her teeth and climbed back into bed. She still felt a little peculiar, but very glad to be alive. Then too, David had never left her. *Never*. Whenever she opened her eyes he had been there, his golden eyes vaguely haunted.

'Sleepy?' He had come back into the room.

'No.' She put out her hand, palm upwards. 'Come and talk to me. You've been very quiet.'

'No wonder.' He sat down on the side of the bed, holding her hand. 'I've never been so frightened in all my life. Come to think of it, I've never *been* frightened. Not like that.'

'You can go to work tomorrow,' she said a little apologetically.

'Can I now?' He glanced down at her. 'The good thing about being the boss is, I can decide that.'

'Then you're not going?'

'No. I can't bear to let you out of my sight.'

'Where's Prince?' She smiled at him, feeling wonderfully happy.

'Where he should be,' he returned dryly. 'Engaging little mutt.'

'With a pedigree a mile long? He never left me.'

'No, he didn't, and that very same night he was served with chicken.'

'Do you love me, David?' From idle chatter she was never more serious in her life.

'*Love* you? God!'

'*Do* you?' she persisted, her heart in her eyes. 'You've never once told me you loved me.'

'Have you told me?' He lifted her hand and pressed it to his mouth.

'That's different,' she said illogically.

'Oh, why?'

'You know I love you. I know nothing about you.'

'That's all nonsense, you know,' he said quietly. 'Surely you knew long ago before we were married, you affected me deeply?'

'Honestly, I didn't.' She gazed at him with worshipping eyes. 'You're so brilliant, and you were older and so much more experienced.'

'Oh, I think you've caught up!' he said dryly, and pressed her palm against his own. 'Let's go back to the other day. I don't ever care to, but we must. I know you had lunch with Morley and I've since found out much of what he had to say.'

'Don't look like that!' she exclaimed. His expression was formidably grim and she even felt sorry for Jon.

'All right.' He smiled. 'I'm transferring him to our Brisbane office. By rights I should sack him, but he seems to be in a mess.'

'So what he told me was a lie.' It wasn't a question, but a sad acceptance.

'Yes.'

'Poor Jon!' she sighed.

'Maybe he'll learn from his mistakes. At least he remembered your saying you were just going for a drive. I thought of the lake as soon as I saw Prince was gone.'

'Thank God!' Catherine exclaimed.

'Jealousy makes people do strange things. Sink to, in Morley's place, contemptible lies.'

'What about Christine?' she reminded him gently. 'She spun quite a few.'

'Ah then, but we know Christine, don't we? I thought better of Jon.'

'He'll be all right!' Catherine drew a quick breath. 'The change may even do him good. Mrs Morley means well, but she's making a lot of mistakes with her son.'

'Let's forget them, shall we?' He looked into her lovely face against the pillows. 'You surely didn't think I married you for anything less than love?'

'Does a man need a son? Who, for instance, would inherit all this?'

'There's you!' He looked at her as though astounded by her reasoning. 'Of course I want a son. In time. I want *you* to myself for quite a while longer. I also want a daughter—no less important to me. You see, darling, plenty of men long for sweet little girls to spoil. There's only one thing, they'll have to look like you.'

Catherine nodded solemnly, her emerald eyes glowing. 'And the boys can look like you.'

'Done.'

'What now?' David looked at her until the colour bloomed softly in her cheeks. Then he laughed and leaned forward to brush her tender mouth. 'Mm, how I love you, but I don't think you're well enough for violent lovemaking.'

'Try me,' she smiled.

'Really, Catherine!'

She thought he would shrug her off teasingly, renouncing what they both wanted, because he thought her too fragile, but there were flames in the golden eyes resting on her. She couldn't even move but looked back into those burnished eyes. They gleamed with love and tenderness and pride and all the while that devastating underlying sensuality.

'It can't possibly harm me,' she said softly. 'In fact you make me strong.'

'Catherine!' He gathered her up to him, bending her like a flower. 'God knows I want to.'

'I'm not an invalid.' Her voice trailed off into a whisper as he bent his head to kiss her throat. 'Love me, darling,' she begged ardently.

'With everything I know!'

He tightened his hold on her and drew her completely into his arms. Her body was wonderfully warm, curving against him where it belonged, and he let his hands trail down to her flawless young breasts.

'I'm going to take you overseas for our honeymoon. We didn't have a proper one. We'll make London our base and see the world together—for real, and so damned romantic!'

'Lovely!' She was pressing little kisses along the line of his jaw. Both of them were breathing deeper, pleasure mounting, catching, like a spark to a fuse. So much tenderness and excitement, pure joy. 'I think I would like to find out who my mother's people were,' she said, voicing a long-held desire.

'Of course, darling,' he said, and began kissing her mouth languorously, so a tremor ran over her whole body. 'One thing,' he added vibrantly, 'whoever they were, they were quality!'.

And so, Catherine was to find out, they were.

Harlequin Romances

The books that let you escape
into the wonderful world of romance!
Trips to exotic places...interesting
plots...meeting memorable people...
the excitement of love.... These are
integral parts of Harlequin Romances—
the heartwarming novels read by
women everywhere.

Many early issues are now available.
Choose from this great selection!

Choose from this list of Harlequin Romance editions.*

*Some of these book were originally published under different titles.

Relive a great love story...
Harlequin Romances 1980
Complete and mail this coupon today!

Harlequin Reader Service

In U.S.A.
MPO Box 707
Niagara Falls, N.Y. 14302

In Canada
649 Ontario St.
Stratford, Ontario, N5A 6W2

Please send me the following Harlequin Romance novels. I am enclosing my check or money order for $1.25 for each novel ordered, plus 59¢ to cover postage and handling.

☐ 422	☐ 509	☐ 636	☐ 729	☐ 810	☐ 902
☐ 434	☐ 517	☐ 673	☐ 737	☐ 815	☐ 903
☐ 459	☐ 535	☐ 683	☐ 746	☐ 838	☐ 909
☐ 481	☐ 559	☐ 684	☐ 748	☐ 872	☐ 920
☐ 492	☐ 583	☐ 713	☐ 798	☐ 878	☐ 927
☐ 508	☐ 634	☐ 714	☐ 799	☐ 888	☐ 941

Number of novels checked @ $1.25 each = $_____

N.Y. State residents add appropriate sales tax $_____

Postage and handling $_____.59

TOTAL $_____

I enclose _____
(Please send check or money order. We cannot be responsible for cash sent through the mail.)

Prices subject to change without notice.

NAME _____
(Please Print)

ADDRESS _____

CITY _____

STATE/PROV. _____

ZIP/POSTAL CODE _____

Offer expires March 31, 1981

009563371